GONE TO GREEN

**Center Point
Large Print**

GONE TO GREEN

Judy Christie

CENTER POINT PUBLISHING
THORNDIKE, MAINE

This Center Point Large Print edition
is published in the year 2010 by arrangement with
Riggins International Rights Services, Inc.

Copyright © 2009 by Judy Christie.

The text of this Large Print edition is unabridged.
In other aspects, this book may vary
from the original edition.
Printed in the United States of America
on permanent paper.
Set in 16-point Times New Roman type.

ISBN: 978-1-60285-641-7

Library of Congress Cataloging-in-Publication Data

Christie, Judy Pace, 1956-
   Gone to green / Judy Christie.
      p. cm.
   ISBN 978-1-60285-641-7 (library binding : alk. paper)
   1. Women journalists--Fiction. 2. Publishers and publishing--Louisiana--Fiction.
   3. Newspaper publishing--Louisiana--Fiction. 4. Louisiana--Fiction.
   5. Large type books. I. Title.
   PS3603.H7525G66 2010
   813'.6--dc22
   2009030582

To my husband, Paul, with love and gratitude

1

Post Media Company announced yesterday that its multimedia division will offer newspaper readers information around the clock, relying on the latest technology and innovation. For more information, see our Web site.

—The Dayton Post

I glanced down at the floorboard and noticed it was Thursday.

Somewhere in the last dozen years or so, I had gotten into the habit of figuring out what day of the week it was by checking the number of coffee mugs rolling around. At least I don't keep tuna sandwiches and an ancient typewriter in the backseat, the way a guy in sports does.

Hurrying into the building, I flashed my security badge at the guard, who reluctantly lifted his head from his Word Jumble puzzle to glance and nod. Let it never be said he didn't get his money's worth out of the daily paper—especially since free papers are one of the perks of working at *The Dayton Post*. He saw me every day, several times a day, but still made me show my badge.

When I hit the front door of the newsroom, I dashed to my desk. I spend a lot of time dashing, especially in the morning when I slide into my cubicle just in time to make eye contact with my staff before the news-planning meeting.

As city editor, I'm in the middle of things, right where I like to be—most of the time. If it weren't for night meetings and procrastinating reporters, this job wouldn't be half bad.

I learned long ago to shape my personal life around my work. That means only occasionally grumbling about the nights and weekends. I'm still a little annoyed about Christmas—I always get stuck working because I'm the one without kids. The schedule's already posted for five months from now, and there I sit: Lois Barker, holiday editor.

"How's it shaping up, Scoop?"

Ed stood in the same spot he stands each morning when I hit the door, waiting to ask what we have for tomorrow's paper. He's the managing editor and has been for a decade. His old-fashioned nickname helps make up for all the annoying jokes I get about my name being Lois and working on the city desk: "How's Clark Kent?" "Feeling mild-mannered today?" "Seen any speeding bullets?"

Ed probably should be the editor by now, but corporate sent in Zach about eighteen months ago—a young, suit kind of bean-counter editor who spends most of his time in accounting meetings.

Zach's a nice enough guy, but he and Ed don't

exactly mesh. Ed thinks Zach is all stick and no carrot.

"Looking good, Ed. Anything special you want us to chase?"

"Just make sure you scrape something up with a little juice to it. And, hey, are you up for some lunch today . . . maybe that sandwich shop down by the library?"

My inner radar spiked into the Red Zone. First of all, it was pork chop day at Buddy's, our favorite spot, just around the corner. Next, Ed and I and a handful of other editors ate lunch together on a regular basis but never made it this formal. Usually we casually gathered at the back door of the newsroom and walked downtown after the noon news on TV.

To set something up in advance was close to an engraved invitation. To choose the mediocre sandwich shop meant he wanted to talk in private.

I frowned. "Sure, I'm good for lunch, but what's up?"

Ed glanced around. In a newsroom someone always lurked with a question, a joke, or to eavesdrop. "I've got some news, but it'll have to wait."

During the news meeting, I watched Ed closely and wondered what he had on his mind. He had been antsy lately—not happy with changes in the paper.

"I don't have anything against corporations owning newspapers," he told me recently, "but I

9

don't like it when they start running newspapers." He was particularly unsettled about the new focus on the Internet and technology. "I didn't get into this business to do podcasts."

Ed threw in a couple of good story ideas during the planning discussion to make sure Zach knew he was paying attention. My best friend Marti, the features editor, tried to keep her top reporter from getting pulled off onto a daily story, and Diane, the business editor, talked in riddles, as though that would somehow impress Zach.

Diane desperately wants to move up and knows Zach can help her get a plum assignment. Thankfully, she hasn't realized it's actually me Zach plans to move up and out. He's supposedly grooming me to be a top editor, not only because he likes me, but because he gets some sort of company points for his promotable employees.

"He gets management stars," Marti said when I told her about my career conversation with Zach a while back. "Or he gets to order a prize out of a catalog with lots of corporate merchandise in it. Maybe you can talk him out of a baseball cap to show off that ponytail of yours."

Admittedly, I'm intrigued by Zach's plans for me. At age thirty-six and still single, it's probably time for me to consider a change.

After we finished the news meeting, Ed herded me out of the conference room. "Let's beat the lunch crowd." It wasn't even 11:30 yet.

"Give me a minute," I said. "Let me get a couple of reporters going on their assignments."

"Hurry up," he said and looked at his watch.

It's a professional habit, but I try to figure things out before people tell me. Ed's secret was killing me. As soon as we hit the door, I tossed my ideas at him. "It's the ad director, isn't it? He really did get fired from his last paper." "Tony's applying for that sports desk position in Atlanta, right?" "Zach's mad at me about that drowning story we missed, isn't he?" Ed wouldn't even look at me. "I can't take this any more! What's up?"

"I've got something to tell you, something big."

"You're scaring me. Tell me."

"I'm going to tell you all of it, but first you have to promise you won't tell anyone, and I mean anyone—not Marti, not your next-door neighbor, not your aunt in Cleveland. This has to stay between us."

Torn between irritation that he seemed to think I'd put this on the Associated Press wire and worry about the bomb he was about to drop, I stopped on the sidewalk. For once, I did not say anything.

He looked at me and smiled big. "I did it."

"Did what?"

"Scoop, I did it! I bought my own newspaper."

"Ed!" I squealed and gave him a quick hug. "Where? When? How? What will I do without you?" I peppered him with the standard journalistic questions and felt that sad, jealous thrill you get when something exciting happens to a good friend.

"Let's get moving, so I can tell you everything without a bunch of ears around."

We started walking, and I tried to smile. "Where? Details, details!"

"*The Green News-Item.* Green, Louisiana— great little town, about seven thousand people. Lots of potential—a big, beautiful lake, a court-house square downtown, major highway on the drawing board."

"Louisiana? You're kidding me. You said you'd go to Oregon or Florida or somewhere like that. Have you ever even been to Louisiana? I mean other than that editors' convention we went to in New Orleans that time?"

"Have now, and I like the feel of the place, Scoop. I realized I didn't want one of those cute places we talked about. This place definitely isn't cute. Besides, if it were, I probably wouldn't be able to afford the paper."

He sort of laughed and groaned at the same time. "This is a family sale. They want to keep Grandpa's paper out of the hands of the govern-ment and Wall Street. It's a twice-weekly: a twice-weekly—bigger than a puny weekly—but an honest-to-goodness newspaper, circulation 4,930, distributed throughout the county . . . I mean, parish. You know, they have parishes in

Louisiana. Green, Louisiana. Bouef Parish. Spelled B-o-u-e-f and pronounced Beff, like Jeff. Weird."

He laughed again.

I had never seen Ed so excited. "They like the looks of me, and I like the looks of them. Most of the family's out of state, too, so I won't have them breathing down my neck. It'll be my paper to do whatever I want with."

As he talked, I thought about what this meant in my life. What would I do without Ed? Whose shoulder would I cry on about being thirty-six and single? Ed is my mentor, friend, and confidante for every piece of good gossip I've picked up in the past decade and a half. The newsroom without him would be like the horrible Thanksgiving when I covered that tornado in Preble County and ate my holiday lunch at a gas station—lousy, just plain lousy.

We turned onto Calhoun Boulevard and headed into the Sandwich Express. I felt a twinge of shame at my selfishness. Ed had wanted to buy his own paper for years now, saving, always reading *Editor & Publisher* to see what was on the market, scouting, working the grapevine. He wanted to put miles between himself and his ex, and he was unhappy with the new corporate policies and his thousand extra duties.

"A twice-weekly," I said. "Busy enough to be a challenge but not the hard work of a daily. In a nice little town. Green, did you say? Sounds like some tree-hugger kind of place." I babbled, collecting my thoughts.

"Very un-tree-huggerish," Ed said. He smiled and shook his head. "But plenty of nice trees."

"Wow. I'm shocked. You actually did it, Ed."

Then I asked the hardest question. "When?"

"I plan to tell Zach this afternoon that I'll stay till after prep football season—give us time to wrap up the projects we've got going. I don't know if he'll want me around that long, though. Lame duck and all. I need to get down there before the end of the year. There's a lot of paperwork and stuff to be done, plus I need to find a place to live."

"Till after prep football season? That's less than two months. Ed, what am I going to do without you?"

"You'll do great, Lois. You'll be out of here within a year anyway. Zach's got you pegged to move onward and upward. I'll be sitting in my dusty office reading about your successes on some corporate PR website. And you can come visit. I may ask you to train my staff—all twelve of them, and that's twelve in the whole building, including the maintenance guy."

My roast beef sandwich sat heavy in my gut, a reminder I need to eat healthier if I'm going to keep the trim figure I'm so proud of. I asked Ed for one of his antacids. He gobbled them by the truckload and complained about losing his appetite in his old age. Between the coffee and the cigarettes, his heartburn was legendary.

"Ed, you know I'm happy for you . . . I really am. I'm going to miss you, though."

We headed back to the newsroom and the official news of the day. Suddenly, my cubicle seemed a little too small and a little too cluttered. The stack of special projects I was most proud of looked yellow and smelled musty. The ivy had more brown leaves than green. My office coffee cup had grown a new layer of mold.

Two fresh memos from Zach were in my mailbox. "Please tell your reporters to quit parking in the visitor lot," and "The city desk needs to increase the number of stories geared to younger readers." As I studied the second note, it pained me to realize I was no longer in the coveted younger reader category.

Ed took the next week off to handle details. "Gone fishing," he wrote on a note posted on his office door. "Back soon."

I moped while he was gone. "Must be a stomach bug," I told Marti, who couldn't figure out what was wrong with me. I hated to mislead her, but there's always a bug going around the newsroom, so it was a fail-safe excuse.

When Ed returned, he hit the highlights of his week over a cup of coffee in the break room. "I made a quick trip to Green and sealed the deal with the owners. The sale remains confidential until I officially take ownership in ninety days. Then the current owners—McCuller is their name—will make some sort of official announcement."

That would be one of those announcements that newspapers hate when other people make, but love it when they do. I rolled my eyes, oddly annoyed.

"I used some investment money and that little inheritance from my folks," he said, "to get things going. And then I took out a whopping line of credit at the local bank. I have a year to start paying for this baby or bail out. Kind of scary."

"Sounds exciting," I said, trying to encourage him, even though it sounded very scary to me.

"There's tons of paperwork. I met with my lawyer here in Dayton and my CPA and got all the particulars taken care of and filed for my retirement pay. I hope Zach will cut me loose—with pay, of course." He laughed. "I'm ready to let my new life begin."

Those were the last words Ed spoke before he passed out right there in the break room.

Within two months, he had left the newsroom all right. My gruff, sloppy, smart, hand-holding friend had died of leukemia. Not one of us had seen it coming.

The weeks of his illness were excruciating for all of us, filled with sadness for our friend and fear for ourselves at how quickly life could turn. I stopped by his house to see him as often as I could, but was ashamed that my visits were mostly hit-and-run efforts.

"Hey, how are things down in Green?" I asked one day, but he changed the subject. I didn't have the heart to try again and ignored the copies of the paper by his couch. Somebody down there must have put him on the mail circulation list; he was too weak to travel.

I was among a handful of people, including Zach, who spoke at the funeral. Somehow I felt Zach had earned that privilege, even though Marti and a few others grumbled about a corporate newcomer charging into our private time. When it mattered most, Zach had treated Ed right.

My comments seemed a bit lightweight—corny stories like the time Ed put a banana on my telephone and called me, so I would pick the fruit up, thinking it was the receiver. I kept my comments short.

"No cry fest and no superhero stuff," Ed told me in one of my final visits with him.

At the service, I surprised myself and several other people by saying a short prayer. "Thank you, God, for the impact of Ed's life. Have mercy on all of us in the days ahead that we might be the people we were meant to be. Amen."

My colleagues and I awkwardly walked away

from the grave. We were good at writing about emotion, but we didn't quite know how to handle it in this first-person version.

I cried all the way back to the newsroom, having designated myself the editor to make sure the Sunday paper got out. Sadness washed over me. Ed had never gotten the chance to live his new adventure, to try out his newspaper, to get out of Dayton and into Green, Louisiana.

His obit had missed the lead. Instead of going on and on about his distinguished career in journalism and how he was nearing retirement and loved to fish, it should have highlighted the new life he had planned. Ed wasn't wrapping up a career. He was about to embark on a Louisiana journey.

As I hit "send" on a story, I saw Zach strolling toward me. Since he usually only phoned in on Saturdays, his appearance surprised me. Sitting on the corner of my desk, he chitchatted about the next day's edition and picked up a paper clip, moving it back and forth between his fingers.

"I appreciated what you said at the funeral, Lois," he said, laying down the paper clip. "I really wish I'd known Ed better, like you did. You did a great job capturing his personality—made me wish I'd taken more time to know what made him tick."

Zach absently rummaged through my candy jar. "Moving around like I have these past few years," he said, "I just haven't gotten to know people deeply the way you knew Ed."

Embarrassed and feeling like I might cry again, I concentrated on my computer screen and deleted old e-mails to avoid eye contact.

"You know, Ed thought the world of you," Zach said. "Told me often how talented you are and how you'd be running your own paper one day. You know that, right?"

I sort of laughed, self-conscious and a little proud. "Oh, Ed liked me because we had worked together forever. He taught me so much."

"Well, I agree with Ed. I want to offer you his job—the managing editor's job." My eyes widened. I closed my computer screen and slowly rolled my chair back. "I beg your pardon?"

"I'd like you to be the next M.E. I've already run it by corporate and gotten their okay."

Rumors had swirled in the newsroom about who would take Ed's place, but this had been one game I'd not let myself get drawn into, mostly because I knew it would mean Ed was truly gone.

Part of me was excited at the idea of a promotion. The other part was annoyed that Zach's plans had been put into motion before he talked to me and that corporate had already signed off on my life.

"Well?" Zach said. "Is that a yes?"

I realized I hadn't given him an answer. I picked up my pencil and doodled on my ever-present reporter's notebook. The ambition in me fought with the fatigue and uncertainty these past weeks had unleashed. Ambition won.

"Thanks, Zach. That sounds great. Thanks. Sure. I'd love to be the M.E." I tried to sound enthusiastic.

"Fantastic!" He leaned over my desk to shake my hand. "I look forward to working more closely with you. I'll iron out the details with HR, and we'll tell the staff within the next week or so."

"Sounds good to me. Thanks again. I guess I'll head on home. I'm pretty tired." A great need to escape engulfed me.

My neat little condo with one puny pink geranium on the patio was about all I could handle at that moment. I walked straight to the bedroom and flopped down on my dark green comforter. I was too beat to think about how my life was about to change.

I briefly considered setting my alarm for church the next day, a habit I had long ago given up. I needed the inspiration, but I could not bring myself to do it.

2

We need your help! The Green News-Item *is happy to tell you we are bringing back our "News-Item Community Items," those nuggets of neighborly news that help us keep up with our friends and family. If you have a tidbit, please give your community correspondent a call. Names and phone numbers are listed on page 2A.*

—*The Green News-Item*

On Monday morning I slid in barely in time to touch base with my reporters. After a flat news meeting—they had all seemed flat these past few weeks—Zach stopped by my desk, told me he needed to talk to me, and motioned me to his office.

Before I could stand up, my phone rang. I groaned inwardly. Good customer service—"service with excellence!"—was more important to Zach than the newsroom management structure. I had better take the call, even though I didn't want to talk to anyone. I wanted to hide under my desk and suck my thumb.

A polite woman asked if I was Lois Barker. "Yes, ma'am, may I help you?" I asked. She had the sound of the women from the monthly clubs who call in their notices instead of mailing them. I opened a computer file and prepared to take the dreaded dictation.

"Good morning, Ms. Barker. I'm the administrative assistant to Attorney Frank Owens. He asked me to call you and make an appointment with him right away to discuss a business matter."

As a journalist, I'm what some might call naturally suspicious. I prefer to think of it as skeptical. No way did I want to chase a news tip or sit through another meeting where a mover-and-shaker complained about one of my reporters. I had met Frank Owens a few years ago at a Rotary Club meeting, and he was a force to be reckoned with in Dayton. "I'm sorry, ma'am, but I'm tied up this week. Could someone else assist Mr. Owens?"

"No, Ms. Barker. Mr. Owens needs to meet with you either today or tomorrow if possible."

I sighed inwardly, set the meeting for first thing the next morning, and headed into Zach's office. But our session was interrupted before we got started by an emergency Executive Committee meeting.

"Sorry, Lois. The E.C. has called a meeting to discuss budget cuts. Before long, you'll be solving these problems for us," Zach said, as he headed off with a legal pad and calculator.

"Ha. Ha," I said out loud to the empty room, wondering what in the world I was getting myself into. I was excited about the promotion—and a little smug that I had passed over the other editors. But I felt like an impostor stepping into someone else's life.

Zach surfaced a couple of times during the day and apologized for canceling on me. I was kind of relieved. In fact, I was so exhausted that if it weren't for the special project I needed to finish, I'd duck out early. "I promise we'll talk first thing in the morning," he said. "The ball is rolling, so you should give some thought as to what will be on your agenda for your first one hundred days as M.E."

Not likely. My brain had already shut down for the day.

The next morning I put on one of my nice doing-business-downtown outfits, feeling remarkably stylish with the way it looked with my long dark hair and brown eyes. I drove to the attorney's office, having found no graceful way to put off the meeting.

I'm not grouchy by nature, but too many people want a piece of me on most days, ranging from the mayor to the school superintendent to lawyers, doctors, and shop owners. I was not looking for-ward to this encounter.

When I walked into the law firm, Frank stood in the outer office, chatting with his secretary. He shook my hand, offered me a cup of coffee that I turned down, and directed me to his executive conference room lined with law books. He pulled out a chair for me.

"Thanks for coming, Lois. I'm sorry for pushing you on this meeting, but there's a deadline involved, and I need to talk with you face-to-face."

Oh, great, a deadline. He had waited until the last minute to do a news release on something and wanted me to get it in. Give me a break. How did I let myself get roped into this? Why don't people just fax me stuff? Annoyed, I almost missed the reason for the meeting.

"This involves your friend Ed. I'm so sorry for your loss," he said, handing me a manila folder. Taking the file, I immediately skimmed the first sheet as he talked.

I'm not quite sure what Frank said after that because I was staring at a copy of Ed's will. Make that Ed's last will and testament, dated about two months ago, on one of the days Ed had taken off work to handle some business.

I glanced up at Frank with what I hoped was a polite, curious smile and looked him in the eye. He smiled back at me.

"As I was saying, Lois, Ed came in here a few months ago to get his business in order. He didn't know he was sick, but he wanted all the loose ends tied up as he closed the deal on the newspaper in Louisiana. He told me he had informed you about his purchase."

"Yes, he was so excited, Frank, but I don't know

what this has to do with me. I need to get back to the newsroom. I don't mean to be crass or anything, but did Ed want me to help with his estate or something?"

"Well, I suppose you could say that, Lois. Ed designated you as the beneficiary of one of his most prized possessions—"

I interrupted him with a big smile. "His Camaro? He left me his 1966 Camaro?"

"I'm afraid not. That went to his next-door neighbor."

"Mr. Hamilton? He's eighty years old—what does he need with a vintage Camaro?" Suddenly, I felt idiotic and shut up. My stomach was churning . . . had been since Saturday.

"Again, Lois, I apologize for rushing you on this meeting. As you might say in the news business, this is a pretty big story. Ed has made you the owner of his newspaper in Green, Louisiana, *The Green News-Item.*"

I stood up and then sat back down before I stood up again. I think I asked for a bottle of water, but I'm not sure.

"Please, Lois, have a seat. I know this must be a shock."

"Frank, you can't be serious. I mean Ed and I were friends and all, but . . . a newspaper!" And then I cried—for that moment when I thought, "I'm rich," and then, "Or am I?" and for my deep sorrow that Ed was gone and for my total confusion.

I took the Kleenex the attorney offered.

Frank sat quietly. The Chamber of Commerce Outstanding Business Leader clock on the conference room wall ticked loudly. Slowly, I picked through my scattered thoughts and found my wits.

"Let me try to understand. Can you walk me through this? What about Ed's brother?"

For a moment Frank looked like he was going to pat me on the head as though I were a small child.

"You may know that Ed and his ex-wife had no surviving children. Their only child died in a car accident twenty years ago. Ed's brother is a missionary in Chile, and I don't think I'm violating Ed's confidence when I say he didn't think the newspaper would be a good fit for a pastor."

I had met Ed's "brother the Father" a handful of times over the years. He was as far from being a journalist as I was from being a missionary.

"But won't he be upset?" I quickly scanned the document in my hand again.

"His brother has been taken care of, Lois. Let's talk about you and your newspaper. The owners want to meet with you as soon as possible. They're a little nervous about this deal and want to wrap it up quickly. Ed agreed that any owner he transferred the paper to would hold onto it for at least a year, allowing for continuity. The owners want to make sure it doesn't revert back to their family."

By the time I left Frank's office two hours later,

I knew three things: Ed was even more of a stand-up guy than I realized, I needed to make the second trip I'd ever taken to Louisiana, and my life had been turned upside down.

I was supposed to keep the paper one year.

Walking slowly to my car, I longed to take the afternoon off so I could think this through. Maybe I could plead a terrible headache and head home. City editors have a weird, overblown sense of duty, though, and I felt bad even considering it. With Ed gone, we were shorthanded and short-tempered as it was. But if I couldn't even take the afternoon off, how could I possibly visit Green and deal with this new drama in my life?

That's when I remembered I'd accepted the managing editor's job, and then the worst headache I've had in ten years hit me—the kind you get when your old boyfriend joins the Peace Corps without you or when the central air unit breaks down on the hottest day of the year. This is the kind of headache that inheriting a newspaper can bring on quickly—a small-town newspaper in the Deep South. Could I handle it for a year?

The headache pounded the words "you took the managing editor's job" over and over in my head. I dug in my purse for my cell phone and called Zach's office with a twinge of desperation.

"He's in a meeting, Lois. Is there something I can help you with?" His secretary was entirely too cheerful.

"Actually, I'm not feeling well and need to go home. Will you give him that message please?"

A million thoughts fought for my attention. "Handle a newspaper in Green, Louisiana, for a year?" "No problem." "Yes, Zach, I'll be your M.E." "Ed, what have you done?" "Thank you, Ed." "I can do this." "I can't do this." I was stunned, excited, queasy, thrilled, and just a little on the edge of insanity.

Driving too fast, I cut through a side street near a local college and, at the last minute, whipped into a parking space. I slipped into the school's charming chapel, one of my favorite local buildings, and took a seat on a back pew. Fall light streaming through the stained glass windows momentarily calmed my fears. Big decisions had to be made in a short amount of time. Where to start?

My mother, who died when I was twenty-five, always said to pray when I needed guidance. In the past few years I had been too busy, too tired, and . . . well . . . too frustrated with the whole God thing to pray. My mother was a deeply spiritual woman, and her death shook me to the core. She would have known how to handle this situation. Tears formed at the corners of my eyes as I thought of how much I missed her.

Each of the chapel's stained glass windows pictured Christ in a Bible story. I focused on one where he was holding a lamb and said, "Help!" My head pounded, and I couldn't sit still.

I sped home, grabbed a can of Diet Dr Pepper, sank down into my overstuffed armchair, and put my feet up on the scratched coffee table I had bought at a flea market. With notebook and pencil in hand, I listed every possible scenario to help me make a decision.

Three hours, four sodas, two bags of hundred-calorie popcorn, and two Tylenol later, I was as confused as ever. My head still pounded.

"Help," I whispered again.

3

What would you buy if you hit the jackpot?
Arlen Wilkes of Route 2 is going to buy an
iPod and load it up with Shania Twain and
Toby Keith songs, after winning $12,000
on a gambling trip to Shreveport.
He wants everyone to know he has already
deposited the money in the bank to
discourage any breaking and entering.
"It ain't in the house," he stressed.

—*The Green News-Item*

Not quite a week after Ed's death, I walked into Zach's office prepared to tell him again how excited I was about the M.E. job and that I needed a few days off to head to Green, Louisiana, to cancel the purchase of the paper Ed had been so excited about.

Since Zach was still in a meeting, I sat at the small table in his office and thumbed through a copy of a management book he had assigned us to read. I was supposed to lead the discussion at next Wednesday's editors' meeting—had already placed the order for our box lunches.

Somewhere between skimming chapter three and noticing the towering, white clouds outside, the word "go" popped into my mind, as though someone had spoken to me, and then said, "I'll help you."

My head whipped around, wondering if anyone else might have heard this. Zach's assistant seemed engrossed in typing calendar listings. No one else was nearby. Maybe I had misheard the police radio, squawking a few feet away near the cop reporter's desk.

I looked outside again and saw a rainbow. I am not making this up. All my doubts and misgivings about letting Ed down and taking the safe way out came rushing back.

"I have some unexpected news," I said to Zach, when he walked in a few minutes later. "I'm giving my notice."

"Real funny," Zach said with a laugh.

"I'm serious. I'm moving down to Louisiana and will see what happens."

"As in run that newspaper?" Zach asked. "You must be pulling my leg. Running a newspaper is hard work and requires intense commitment." He grew more heated with every passing moment.

"Have you forgotten I help run this newspaper twelve to fourteen hours every day? I'm fully aware of what's involved." I was bluffing. My resignation surprised me as much as Zach.

"You're committing career suicide, Lois. Leaving now would be a huge mistake."

I took a deep breath, noticing it sounded shaky when I exhaled. "I might be . . ." My voice weakened. Then I sat up straighter. "But I have to give this a try."

"Go, then," Zach said, standing up. "But I expect you to stay through the holidays. You know how tough it'll be to find a good city editor, especially one who wants to move this time of year."

"Are you saying you want thirty days notice?"

"Thirty days with a few stipulations, Lois," he said in his manager's voice. "Your departure will put us in a bind. I insist you pick up the slack over the holidays, and that means no extra time off." He glanced at a folder on his desk. "You'll be due a year-end bonus, and I'll help you get it, but only if you agree to my terms. No time off."

He was clearly annoyed I had backed out on the new job. Feeling a bit guilty about it, I agreed.

It was that simple. The course of my life changed in twenty minutes, without writing one word in a notebook or bouncing it off Marti or talking to my CPA. I thought I had heard the word "go," and I was going to Green to figure out how to run a little newspaper and change my life.

My plans to move to Green, a place I had never set foot in, took shape via FedEx and long distance calls. I put off the McCuller family until after the New Year, but not without some strain. My contact with them was limited mostly to Iris Jo, a distant cousin who was the bookkeeper and apparently not part of the rich side of the family. She sent me financial statements, a market profile, and copies of the newspaper.

"They want you to know this is all highly irregular," she said, sounding a bit apologetic. "The paperwork has been redone for you to take ownership on January 1. They would have preferred you to come down for a face-to-face and sign the documents." She hesitated. "The McCullers asked me to tell you they're ready to get on with the deal. Call me anytime. I'll be glad to help you anyway I can. Chuck and Dub McCuller will meet with you at four o'clock on the first day of the New Year, January 1," Iris Jo said. "They wanted me to tell you to please be prompt."

"Am I crazy?" I asked Marti at lunch that day.

"I don't think so," she said, not quite the reassurance I had hoped for.

"Gone to Green," I wrote on a sheet of paper with a black marker, giving my cell phone number and e-mail address. "Stay in touch." I taped it to

32

the newsroom mailboxes and walked out of the Dayton newspaper, wanting to laugh and cry.

I pulled out of my garage at 10:45 a.m. on New Year's Eve, my car loaded down with everything I hadn't entrusted to the movers. My belongings had been put into a big load with two other families' precious things, to be dropped off at some undetermined time. I hoped I would see my stuff again and that my green pottery collection wouldn't be unloaded at the Smith family home in Peoria. I also hoped I wasn't making the worst mistake of my life.

An odd, fast-motion account of my adult life unwound in my mind as I drove out of Dayton. I wondered yet again what Ed had been thinking when he wrote my name in his will on the same line as the *The Green News-Item*.

Pulling into Green in the middle of the next afternoon, with the official newspaper meeting fast approaching, I had absolutely no idea what I was doing.

"The quaint lakeside town I had pictured does not exist," I said to Marti, during an SOS call from the car. "Obviously, whoever did the Chamber's Web site is a master at good lighting and interesting angles and hyperbole."

"Maybe you can hire them for the paper," she said, trying to sound supportive. I could hear the sounds of a football game in the background and remembered she had invited a few of our friends over.

"The outskirts of town look like an ad for fast-food franchises and stores where everything costs a dollar. It's horrible. What have I done? I want to go home."

"Lois Barker, you'll be fine. You always are. Now, pull yourself together. Call me back later when you know more. I'm having a terrible time hearing you."

Desperate to find a real neighborhood, I turned down a small side street with potholes big enough to suck up my car. Several overturned garbage cans spilled out a week's worth of trash on the sidewalks, and candy wrappers and soft drink cans littered the front yards of the small, shabby houses.

I had imagined driving into a sweet town with children dressed in colorful sweaters riding their bikes. Instead, junk cars rusted in front yards, and upholstered furniture decorated more than one porch. The area looked like something out of a Third-World country. Only a few houses were halfway neat and adorned with old tires, cut and painted white to make flowerbeds.

People stared at me, and I stared back. I resisted the urge to roll down my window and explain that I was the new owner of the paper. My urgent need to get out of that place surpassed the desire to interact.

After a couple of wrong turns, I did a stealth drive-by of the newspaper building. It had a sort of noble, forlorn look, with one battered pickup parked in the lot. I squinted and saw that it had "News-Item, No. 1" painted on it.

Downtown was deserted except for a teen-age girl who lounged on a bench outside the paper, smoking a cigarette. The small surge of pride I had felt at surveying my domain was sullied by worries about how to deal with stray people who hung around the loading dock.

The area near the paper included a barbershop with a sign that read "Jesus Saves"; a Ford dealership, proudly proclaiming itself the smallest in the South; an antique mall, advertising booths for rent; and a small local department store. I already knew the store and car dealership were important in my life. Iris Jo had told me over the phone that they were among the biggest advertisers in the paper, and both were owned by one of the richest families in town.

Right on the dot of four o'clock, I knocked on the front door of my inheritance for someone to let me in. A trim woman, about my age and dressed in blue jeans and a fleece pullover, opened the door.

"Lois?" she asked in a soft southern voice. "Welcome. I'm Iris Jo. I've been looking forward to meeting you in person. Follow me, please." I was momentarily astonished. The way she spoke on the phone, I had expected a woman in her sixties.

She led me into a 1970s style boardroom decorated with a couple of paintings of English foxhunts, a faded silk fern, and a huge conference table occupied by the two McCuller men who were to help me make the transition. Both men had thinning gray hair, but Chuck appeared to be the older of the two—somewhere in his early sixties. His portly stomach strained against his knit shirt and the waistband of his burgundy polyester pants, and his blotchy red face looked like he drank too much. Dub stopped short of being thin, but at least he wore up-to-date pressed jeans and a button-down blue oxford shirt. His smile came more frequently than his brother's.

"Well, you're a lot younger and prettier than that friend of yours," Dub said as I approached. "Taller too."

While Dub was prone to chitchat, Chuck seemed to be in charge and plunged right in. His only advice amounted to telling me who in the community I needed to be extra nice to. "You want to treat your advertisers right. Let them know you're part of the community. Don't make waves."

"Treat them right," Dub repeated.

"Make sure they know the paper appreciates them," Chuck continued. "Needs them. Major Wilson, Eva Hillburn, a handful of others—very important to the paper."

Dub pointed to two boxes on the big table and quickly walked me through a few files, telling me to let Iris Jo know if I had questions.

At this point, I had nothing but questions—about my newspaper, my life, my sanity. I smiled and said "thanks" and headed out for a tour of the building with Iris Jo. Entering the cavernous pressroom, I squinted in the dim light and breathed the familiar smell of newsprint and ink. Pallets of sales flyers lined one end of the room, waiting to be inserted, a good sign for my bottom line.

"This is our cranky old letter press," Iris said. "It's called Bossy because it determines if the paper gets out. No press, no paper. And this is the mailroom where papers are prepared for delivery."

She walked me through a messy coffee station near what might be called the newsroom, tiny compared to Dayton's, with four desks and a small TV. "Our staff is no doubt smaller than you're used to," she said, "but you've got good, hard-working folks here."

The two former owners, who had pawed through a filing cabinet in the office while we were gone, had a few files in their hands when Iris handed me a big batch of keys, sorted in white envelopes labeled "front door," "McCuller office," and "miscellaneous." Holding those keys, with no pomp and little circumstance, I truly became the owner of *The Green News-*

Item. I shook hands with the unenthusiastic Hoss and Little Joe and agreed to meet them at eight the next morning for the announcement to the staff.

"We've got you all set for the next few days at the Lakeside Motel and Marina," Iris Jo said. "The owners are small advertisers and willing to do a trade with the paper for your room. I think you'll like this better than the new chain motel on the other side of town. That one's more suited for out-of-towners here to attend a funeral or wedding."

She handed me directions. "It's easy to find. Call me tonight if you need me."

I nodded and walked out, anxiety washing over me.

Not surprisingly, the Lakeside, on the banks of Bayou Lake, was old and slightly rundown. Its neon sign proclaimed, "Nice Rooms, Good View." A note taped to the front door for "Ms. Barker, News-Item" told me Room Eight was unlocked and mine for the next five nights. By now it was nearly dark outside, and the parking lot lights appeared to be burned out or turned off for the evening.

Sticking my head inside the room, I flipped on the light. To my surprise, the space was tidy and fairly modern. A small welcome basket with bottled water, cheese crackers, and an apple sat on the dresser. A note welcomed me in the same beautiful script as the one that had directed me to this room. They might not be much on desk service, but they sure had good penmanship.

My first order of business was to call Marti back. When she picked up the phone, I burst into tears. "It's ugly," I said. "It's dirty and ugly. The old owners are condescending, and the downtown looks abandoned. What have I done?"

Marti immediately shifted into her logical mode. "Now, Lois, calm down. Don't you think it'll look better by light of day?"

"I got here by light of day. It looks terrible. This town needs a makeover worse than I do."

"Aren't you proud of yourself for getting out of Dayton? And taking care of Ed's pet project? You're going to do great. You're just tired. You've had a full day."

Her encouraging words and familiar laughter did help. Slowly, I began to feel better.

"What would your mother say?" Marti asked. She had known my mother for only a couple of years but had loved her and often brought up her memory. Mom had appreciated the fact that Marti "kept an eye on me."

"She'd say for me to pray about it and get a good night's sleep. And to keep my hairbrush and panty hose clean."

"Okay, then what are you going to do?"

"Cry and head back to Dayton."

"Not the answer I wanted to hear."

"I guess I'll scrounge up a burger and hit the sack. Tomorrow I have to march into that building and meet a group of people who probably won't like me and figure out how to make money out of this newspaper. On second thought, maybe I will pray. Talk to you tomorrow. And, Marti, don't tell Zach."

If I was going to suffer, I sure didn't want him to know.

4

LuAnn Torti, director of the local feline rescue society, was knocked unconscious this week by a cat who pushed an antique pitcher off LuAnn's refrigerator, striking the animal lover on the back of the head. "She's a sweet kitty and never would intentionally hurt anyone," LuAnn said, holding an icepack to her hair and petting her baby with her other hand.

—The Green News-Item

After taking advantage of both cups of coffee in the tiny pot in the room—one regular, one decaf— I replaced my pajamas with sweats and a T-shirt and stepped outside.

The darkness of night still surrounded the Lakeside. I was definitely the only one stirring on day two of the New Year. The wind down here in

North Louisiana was colder than I had expected. It blew off Bayou Lake with a dampness that ate into my midwestern bones. The complete darkness confused me, and I went back into the room to double-check the clock radio. It was, indeed, nearly 6:30 a.m.

I grabbed a jacket and sat down in the plastic Adirondack chair on my small porch, curious and scared about what the day and the new year would bring.

Slowly, a deep red sliver appeared. The sky exploded with pink and orange as the sun rose over the lake, a scene right out of a Louisiana travel brochure. Cypress trees grew everywhere, and Spanish moss glowed in the morning light. At least, I thought they were cypress trees because they had those odd knobby roots growing around them. They jogged a memory from a family vacation to Florida in third grade.

Preparing for the first day at my new job, I deliberately chose the same outfit I had worn the day I learned about Ed's gift to me. The symbolism gave me much-needed optimism—a professional suit of armor as I headed into battle. The newspaper business is my life, but this morning I felt like a rank amateur.

Nervously, I gathered my notebook and file folders into my briefcase and accidentally picked up the Gideon Bible from the bedside table. I flipped it open and my eyes went directly to the word "wisdom." I read the verse. "If anybody lacks wisdom, ask God, and it will be provided. Believe and do not doubt."

I was full of doubts.

Driving into the newspaper, I took the most direct route. Today was not a day for sightseeing. Besides, I was afraid if I detoured at all, I might hop up on the highway, head to the interstate, and never look back. When I arrived, I bypassed the "Publisher" spot in the rough parking lot, as well as one of three visitor spaces still open, and parked in the back near *The News-Item* No. 1 truck. No doubt it was the pride of my fleet. I dug in my purse for my envelopes of keys, fished out the front door key, and stumbled on the steps in the process. Looking up, I noticed a list of about a half-dozen names painted on the window in that kind of paint that high schools use for pep rallies. What in the world?

I stooped to pick up the copies of the day's *Baton Rouge Morning Advocate* and *New Orleans Times Picayune*, the big-city papers from down the road, thrown on the steps. The rolled-up newspapers were oddly comforting—a ritual at newsrooms across the country and a fix for news junkies.

Juggling the newspapers, my envelopes of keys, my briefcase and purse, I struggled with the door and nearly fell inside just as someone unlocked it for me. This was not the entrance I planned, nor the encounter the startled desk clerk expected.

"May I help you?" she asked in a slightly aggravated Southern voice, with about the same enthusiasm I had given unexpected newsroom callers at my former job.

"Oh, hello, good morning . . . I'm Lois Barker, here to see Dub and Chuck McCuller." This was not the time to mention I was her new boss, and that I hated the amateurish painting on the front window.

The woman, in her late twenties, didn't offer her name and gave me a look that said I must be kidding. "Mr. Dub and Mr. Chuck don't usually get in quite this early," she said. "I'd say they won't be here for another hour or so. Could someone else help you?"

At that moment, I wanted to declare myself emperor, march past her, and take control of my office, my paper, my destiny. I longed for the snippy guard at my former newspaper. But I rather nervously said, "Any chance Iris Jo is around, or might I wait in the boardroom?"

The clerk led me begrudgingly into the archaic room, stopping to grab the phone at the counter on the way. She neglected to show me that I had to push a small latch to get through the swinging gate, and my legs hit hard before I realized my mistake.

When she left me in the boardroom, she closed the door behind her, as though I might escape and

43

ransack the building. I deliberately pulled out the heavy chair at the head of the table and settled in, anxiously arranging files to look official and to feel as though I belonged here, even though I was alone in the room.

Give me wisdom. The unspoken prayer came from some unexpected spot.

For the next few minutes, I looked at the odd foxhunt paintings and decided to replace them with photos from the newspaper. I wondered if there was an executive restroom for my use and my use only. When Iris Jo came in, I wanted to hug her—and chide her for not being there before me.

"Welcome back," she said. "Can I get you a cup of coffee?"

Drinking coffee together at the large table, we went over the day's plans. "I expect the McCullers any minute now. They've planned a building-wide gathering in the newsroom/composing room for 8:15," she said. "They'll announce the sale of the paper to you and take questions."

The brothers waltzed in late, with no apology. "Let's get this show on the road," Chuck said impatiently, as though I had held him up. He left the boardroom and turned right to walk down a short hall, Dub one step behind. I fell into line, my heart thudding in my chest.

The announcement was a bit more dramatic than the passing of the keys the previous day—but not by much. Just over half of the staff of twelve showed up. Two were out in the field selling ads, one was on sick leave following hernia surgery, and one was on a duck-hunting vacation. The crowd was small.

Iris Jo brought chocolate and glazed Southern Girl doughnuts, apparently a newspaper tradition for special occasions. She passed them out as we gathered, with Dub and Chuck shaking hands and chatting before becoming more official.

"Morning, everyone," Dub said. "Hope you all had a good holiday. My brother and I are here to tell you this morning that we've made a few New Year's resolutions. We plan to spend more time on the lake and in the woods."

The staffers laughed. I scanned the room in search of a friendly face.

Chuck jumped in. "After much thought, the McCuller family has decided to sell *The Green News-Item*, and we are happy to introduce you to the new owner—Miss Lois Barker. This pretty lady is an editor from a big newspaper up north and is ready to roll up her sleeves and get to work. She comes highly recommended."

I stared at him, wondering if he had actually checked me out and bemused by his use of the word "pretty."

The announcement seemed to be a surprise . . . and not the good kind of surprise. The young woman from the front desk groaned softly. The pressman, easily identified by his stained jump-suit, gave Iris Jo a questioning look. The one person wearing a tie kept glancing over at the McCullers and then down at the floor.

The only newsroom person who had made the meeting raised his hand immediately. "Do you expect to make any staff changes?"

Before I could answer, he threw two more questions at me. "Have you ever been to Green before? Will you consider increasing the amount the staff gets paid for mileage?"

"Now wait a minute, son, before you start interrogating her," Chuck said. "First we want to tell you that things are not going to change. Our *News-Item* will continue to uphold the fine traditions it always has. Everyone's job is safe. Isn't that right, Miss Lois?" He winked when he turned to me and then looked back at the staff. "And if she gets too frisky, y'all just give me and Dub a call, and we'll come right over and make everything right."

Uneasiness ran through me at the joking threat. I wondered if the McCullers might remain a bit more involved than expected.

"I'm so happy to be here," I said in the world's shortest acceptance speech. "I look forward to working with each of you. Thank you, Dub and Chuck and the rest of your family, for your years of stewardship of this paper and this community. We wish you all the best and hope you'll keep your subscription to the paper and that LSU always wins."

People laughed nervously. Iris Jo and the woman from the lobby applauded.

I slowly walked around the group, shaking hands, chatting, trying to remember names, and avoid sticky doughnut crumbs.

The man in the tie introduced himself as Lee Roy Hicks. "I handle advertising and circulation," he said, "and I look forward to going over the numbers with you." His tone didn't quite match his words, though, and his handshake was one of those half handshakes that I learned Southern businessmen gave women.

The "Big Boys" did not stick around long and handed me off to Iris Jo but stressed that Lee Roy was "my go-to guy." I suspected Iris Jo ran the place, and I'd be going to her a lot more than to Lee Roy.

Walking into my rather ornate, if somewhat outdated, office did feel good. I sat at the desk and prepared to check my e-mail—until I realized I didn't have a computer. I began a to-do list.

A timid knock sounded at the door, and the front-lobby warrior walked in—Tammy, I now knew her name to be. She had already apologized for not being more helpful that morning, but it was fairly clear she thought I should have told her who I was and what I was doing there.

"Miss Lois," she said, "can I ask you a quick question?"

Among the things I learned that day was that despite all my best efforts, I would be "Miss Lois" to seventy-five percent of the people I encountered, and Tammy was the master of the "quick question." She walked into my office and stood before a chair, not speaking for the moment.

"It's Tammy, right?" I motioned for her to sit down. "What's on your mind?"

"I was wondering," she hesitated, fiddling with her chunky necklace. "Would it be okay if I buy a new stapler for the front counter?"

A new stapler? I signed off on staplers?

"Of course, Tammy. Get whatever you need."

"Just one more quick thing, if you've got a minute." An attractive woman in her twenties, she fidgeted in the chair, almost like a high school student in the principal's office. Her clothes looked inexpensive, but she wore them well.

"Sure." I nodded.

"Well, I usually take my lunch from noon till one every day. I like to watch *All My Children* while I eat my turkey sandwich. Is that going to be a problem?" By now she was so nervous she fiddled with her fingernails.

Tammy's questions made me antsy, cementing the scope of my new job. I was responsible for the next day's front page—and for making sure we had the proper car advertising and that the grocery store inserts got in? And setting lunch hours for the staff?

"Whatever you've been doing, just keep doing it for now," I said.

"Do you watch any soap operas, Miss Lois?"

I shook my head and stood up. I did what any self-respecting new newspaper owner would do. I decided to leave the building. "I guess I'd better get going," I said. "Have a good afternoon, Tammy."

She looked perplexed as I walked out to Iris Jo's desk.

"Do you think you could show me the house the McCullers offered for the year?" I asked my new assistant. The rent-free house had come up at the last minute, part of the package when the Big Boys were trying to entice me to Green in a hurry. Seeing it had suddenly risen on my priority list.

Slightly frazzled, Iris Jo explained in her kind way that she did not have time for the jaunt. "I would love to go with you, but I just don't see how I can. I'm still trying to close out the books for the year and am a little behind, what with all the changes. May I see your keys, please?"

Digging around in my envelopes, she fished out a key. "Do you think you might take a look by yourself? Or, I could ask Tammy to take you. She might be able to get away."

Riding with Tammy would thwart my escape, so I took the key. "No problem," I said. "I can check it out on my own. It'll help me get the lay of the land."

"Here's how to get there," Iris said. She jotted down directions that included a gravel road, a house trailer with three dogs in the front yard, and a small church. I immediately surmised I was not being offered one of the famed McCuller condos on the lake.

During the past seventy-two hours I had beaten myself up pretty good for my lack of preparation for this move, including nailing down a place to live. I had to keep reminding myself I had done the best I could—saying goodbye, covering holiday shifts, studying my new paper.

"Thanks, Iris Jo, for all your help. I'll be fine." My words were more confident than my spirit at that moment.

As I walked through the building, Alex, the reporter in a pair of torn jeans and a faded T-shirt, stopped me and asked for my bio and a quote or two for the news announcement the next day. "I'd like to take a mug shot of you before you get away too."

I was embarrassed that I had not even thought of the story for the paper. My journalism skills were already slipping.

I sat down for a quick interview and typed out some quotes, not trusting him to get it right. "Don't we have a photographer on staff?" I asked, knowing I had seen a name on the payroll sheets, in addition to a parking spot labeled "Photographer."

"Oh, yeah," Alex said. "He works part-time and takes photos for advertising and news. I think he's out shooting some houses for the real estate pages today. I usually shoot my own art. Unless it's a really big story, you know."

It took only a split second for him to realize that didn't sound right. "I mean breaking news, you know, spot news, that kind of stuff. We can handle mugs, portraits, whatever you want to call them."

So I stood in the front of the building and let Alex shoot me. He chattered as he snapped away, with the blunt speech of most young reporters. "I've been at the paper about six months and appreciate being part of your farm club. This will serve me well when I get ready to move to a bigger paper. I can learn a lot from a woman owner from out of state. A new perspective, you know."

He snapped another photo and glanced at his watch. "Well, got to go. Time for the police jury meeting." Before I could collect my thoughts, he sprinted to his car, with his tennis shoes slapping the pavement.

I walked slowly into the building and stopped to ask Tammy my own quick questions. "Tammy, what is a police jury meeting? And why do we have a list of names painted on the window?" The list had grown by two since I came in that morning.

"The police jury, they're like the governing

body of the parish, you know, Bouef Parish. Green's the parish seat for Bouef Parish. We don't have counties down here in Louisiana." She sort of drawled out the word "Louisiana" in a nice way, in between hemming and hawing. "You probably know it's spelled B-o-u-e-f, but it's pronounced Beff, kind of like the name Jeff." I remembered Ed telling me the same thing and felt my throat tighten.

"Anyway, the police jury runs lots of legal announcements—good money for us and sometimes some juicy stuff in there. You just wouldn't believe who don't pay their taxes." She took a breath. "Lately, they've been discussing a new subdivision or something that Major Wilson and his group want to develop on the lake. Not quite sure about all that."

Tammy paused to pick up the phone, hitting one of two lines and sounding quite pleasant to the person who wanted to place a wedding announcement in the paper.

"How much do we charge for those?" I asked when she got off. She looked surprised.

"Charge? For weddings? What do you mean? They're free." I could tell my question had set off a mild panic, as though we were about to end a centuries long tradition and cheat people out of their right to be in the paper for free. I was considering just that.

I asked again about the names painted on the

window. I had never seen anything like it, and I could not figure it out, which bugged me.

"Oh, those are people who have died since the paper came out," she said, matter-of-factly. "Funeral homes fax them in from all over the area. I put them up there every day so people will know who they need to visit at the funeral home, get their food ready, that sort of thing. I mean, I do it every weekday . . . not weekends. Tom in the newsroom usually comes in on weekends to post them. You'd be surprised how many folks come by to take a look every day."

Then, as if remembering my question about paid weddings, she said, "It's a real community service . . . and we run their obits in the paper on Tuesdays or Fridays. That's free too. Birth announcements too. You know, Miss Lois, everyone ought to get their name in the paper for free when they are born, get married, and die. And we do wedding anniversaries for free, too, from twenty-five years on up."

I now owned and had to make a profit from a paper that offered free everything and painted a list of death notices on the front window. Perhaps I should revisit my prayer for wisdom.

5

*Green police made a traffic stop on Main
Street after several 911 calls that a Mercedes
Benz was driving erratically and there
appeared to be no one at the wheel. Upon
stopping the car, police discovered the driver
was a seven-year old who had taken his
father's car for a spin in retaliation for his
dad not buying him a new skateboard.
No arrests were made.*

—*The Green News-Item*

In my mind, my new home was a nice little rental
cottage within a couple of miles of the paper. I
was surprised, therefore, when Iris Jo's directions
led me out to one of the main highways, away
from the lake, and away from civilization as best
I could tell. There were lots of woods everywhere—piney woods they were called in the
regional advertising materials—a deserted cotton
gin, and what looked to be agricultural acreage
and ponds with pumps in them.

I found Grace Community Chapel and turned
onto the gravel road and past the "house where the
new lady preacher lives" and the "coach's trailer
with three dogs in the front yard." I passed another
pond or two and then a tidy house on the right,

with green shingle siding. A small fake windmill sat in the front yard, and a fishing boat was parked to the side. Iris Jo had told me she lived there.

Slowly, I drove "exactly two miles" down the road, hoping not to ding my windshield and looking for a mailbox labeled Route 2, Box 32. "My" house would be sitting back a piece on the left, according to Iris Jo, and would have a screened porch, a garage, and a big cottonwood tree in the side yard. The house belonged to Aunt Helen McCuller—"Ain't" Helen as the local people pronounced it, a woman who had gone to the nursing home a year or so ago. One of the McCuller kids had lived there for a while before moving to Dallas to take a CPA job. It had been vacant since.

Turning in, my heart rose and sank. "Quaint" might be the word to describe the place. In the midst of winter, brown grass covered the yard, and dead plants lined the flowerbeds. Beautiful bushes loaded with small pink flowers offered the only bright spot. The garage listed to the right, close to falling down, but the house itself looked decent.

Opening the front door with the same fortitude with which I had entered the Lakeside Motel the evening before, I was amazed at how chilled a vacant house in winter could be. A musty smell hit me. This was not the awful been-empty-for-years smell but one of fairly recent paint and what was probably Louisiana dampness. As I wandered through, I noted with delight the wood floors and with dismay the space heaters and ancient avocado appliances.

In the war of emotions I had waged for weeks now, I won a minor victory here, although I had to quickly analyze it. The house offered free rent for a year but was located too far from town. The surroundings were peaceful but sort of desolate. My antiques would look great scattered about, even if the house was a little worn around the edges.

The free rent for a year made up my mind. I could live here for my year in Green, honor Ed's original commitment, and not leave the paper in the lurch. I also needed to consider my own future in this house. The beautiful lakeside properties I'd seen in the real estate guide enticed me, but money factored into my choice to stay here.

Then a large rat ran across the kitchen.

I hate rats. I can abide spiders—even snakes—but I hate rats. I looked around for something to jump up on. My theory on rats is if you see one, there are probably a couple dozen more waiting to jump out. Nearly running to my car, I considered other housing options, such as living for a year at the Lakeside or rooming with Iris Jo or Tammy. But I could not live out here in the middle of nowhere, surrounded by fields, forests, and rodents. I started the motor, and if there'd been asphalt, I would have burned rubber out of the driveway.

Totally caught up in my housing dilemma, it took a few seconds to register that my car sounded as though a helicopter had landed on it. It limped to the side of the narrow road, and I got out, hoping I was far enough away from the trailer that the dogs wouldn't chase me. I'm one of the few people in the world who will admit to not being a dog person. I also confess to a deathly fear of dogs, from terriers to pit bulls and all models in between.

My quick inspection confirmed a flat tire. Shivering in the cold wind and dressed only in my favorite business suit and boots, I looked around. I was stranded in the boondocks within sight of a yard with three big dogs. I punched in the office number on my cell phone, hoping that *News-Item* truck No. 1 might take me back to town. But this was the outskirts of Green, Louisiana, and my cell phone had no reception—not one bar.

I assessed my options yet again. I could drive on the bad tire until I reached town, probably ruining the rim; drag out the jack and spare tire and try to change my first tire ever; or I could walk toward town in hopes of finding help.

I chose the latter. Maybe someone would be at the little church.

Luck was on my side. An older-model green Taurus was parked behind the church. I know all makes of cars. It's a weird, somewhat useless base of knowledge. I suppose it might come in handy someday if I'm in a car chase or witness a bank robbery getaway. I walked around the churchyard, calling "hello," hoping the preacher's family didn't own a dog and wishing I had not left my jacket in the car.

No one answered at the house, but the side door of the church was unlocked. As I entered the dimly lit sanctuary, a distinct cozy smell greeted me. I was standing up near the choir loft, and beautiful winter light streamed through the stained glass windows. The sight shook me. How long ago that day in the college chapel seemed, even though it had only been a handful of weeks. Life could change fast.

I called out "hello" a bit louder and wandered behind the sanctuary, where there was a room with a little table and tiny chairs for children; a fellowship hall with a large coffee maker; and a small paneled office. A woman wearing a souvenir sweatshirt for a walk-a-thon sat at the desk, looking over notes. An open Bible lay nearby.

The woman jumped when I tapped on the door. "Sorry, I do that every time. I'm still not used to being in this building by myself." She looked like she was going to hug me but then held out her hand. "Jean, Jean Hours, Pastor Jean Hours." I could not say why, but it felt good to shake hands as I introduced myself and explained my predicament.

"May I use your phone, Pastor? I don't seem to have cell service out here."

"No problem," she said, moving the phone on her desk my way. "You might as well toss that cell phone. Green is notorious for weak service. But I can take care of that flat for you. I've had lots of experience lately changing tires. I've had two flats in the past six months, and one of my church members had one last week when she dropped off a cake at my house."

I tried to turn down her offer, but was glad when she would not take no for an answer. She grabbed a denim jacket hanging nearby and headed outside through a back door.

"I think God's trying to teach me something with all these tires," she said with a laugh. "I don't know—humility, patience, remembering not to be too full of myself."

She dug around in my trunk and pulled out the tiny spare and jack. "Let's see if we can find the key to unlock the lug nuts."

"I should know where that is." I leaned over beside her without a clue what she was talking about.

"Here we go." She held up a small piece of metal and knelt by my car.

I stepped back, unsure what to do. "I'm so sorry for bothering you. I know you have better things to do than roll around in the dirt for a stranger."

"I welcome the interruption," she said, breathing heavily as she hoisted the tire onto the car. "It's so quiet out here, and I was trying to pull together a sermon. It just wasn't working—a passage from James, maybe you know it, on depending on God for wisdom, on holding your tongue. I'm struggling with it—you know, new preacher jitters."

"Well, I'm not much of a Bible scholar," I said, trying to make a joke. "But I learned about it in Sunday school, I think, when I was a kid." I didn't mention I'd read the same verses that very morning in my hotel room Bible.

I handed the preacher the lug nuts, and she chatted as she tightened them. "What brings you out to Route 2 on this cold day anyway?"

"Just looking around. I'm new to the area and heard about a vacant house out here."

"You probably mean Helen McCuller's place down the road. Nice old house. This is a great community," she said. "Seems like it's out in the middle of nowhere, but it's a tight little neighborhood." Jean dusted off her hands and wiped a little grease onto her jeans. "Probably want to get your tire fixed right away," she said. "That little bitty doughnut spare is like a temporary crown on your tooth—not good for many miles."

"Thank you so much," I said. "I don't know what I would have done if you hadn't been here. You're the first person who ever volunteered to change a tire for me."

"Happy to help. Come on in, and I'll make us a cup of hot chocolate."

I followed her into the house behind the church, unable to figure out a way to politely decline. My heels sank into the gravel driveway.

"Welcome to my humble parsonage," she said. "Isn't that funny? I live in a parsonage. There's something just a little odd about getting a free house next door to your office."

This house reminded me of Helen's down the road, except without any sign of rats. The place was comfortable but needed work. Jean was sheepish about several pieces of furniture, including a monstrosity of a fake-wood wall unit in the living room and a large fancy dining room suite.

"Nice, eh?" she said, giving me a quick tour. "The church won't let me move those out. They bought them for their former preacher as a gift of love to be left in the parsonage when he moved, of course. He retired up to Hot Springs and couldn't care less about this furniture anyway." She looked around, as though someone might overhear. "I hate it, but I figure that battle will have to wait."

She fixed our cocoa in old Fiesta Ware cups that I loved. "Tell me about what brings you to Green," she said.

I told her about inheriting *The Green News-Item*. She was clearly fascinated about my ownership of the paper and my "bold new adventure," as she referred to it.

Visiting with this pastor made me happy because I could avoid going back downtown for a while. She was enthusiastic about my move, as though she had known me for years and was celebrating my great success at something I had worked hard for.

"You're going to do great," she said. "You'll be a breath of fresh air for the Green community."

A little uncomfortable with her goodwill, I began asking her questions, an interview disguised as conversation. In the next thirty minutes or so, I learned more about Jean than I had known about most of my neighbors in the past few years.

"I spent more than twenty years as a schoolteacher in Baton Rouge—high school English," she said, smiling, "wrestling hormonal teenagers to learn about literature. Loved it."

"Why'd you leave?" I was as curious about her as she seemed about me.

"A call from the Lord. He wanted me to be a preacher, and I have to tell you, I resisted for quite some time. It was hard. I knew how to be a teacher, but this . . . this really uprooted me."

She was rewarded in her new calling by being assigned to this small, dying church in rural North Louisiana about eight months ago. Oddly, she didn't seem to hold a grudge for the location or the size of the congregation, although it was clear she was trying to find her way. She sprinkled her conversation with remarks about how God was blessing her on this journey, despite what she called some "dry bones" moments.

"The hardest part has been being away from my husband," she said. "Believe it or not, I'm forty-eight years old, and this is the first time I've ever lived alone. Married the week after I graduated from college. He's still in Baton Rouge, has a good job at a bank there, and . . ." Her voice trailed off, and her eyes narrowed, as though she were looking at something in the distance.

"Will your husband move here too?" The reporter in me couldn't help but ask the obvious question.

"He hasn't been able to make it yet. Comes here when he can and keeps an eye on things there—the house, the kids. Our daughter's in college in Lafayette. Our son works in Baton Rouge and has an apartment."

For the first time, Pastor Hours seemed unsure. "That's been the straw that broke the camel's back for my new church. It was bad enough to get a woman preacher, and then she turns up without her husband." She clasped her hands in front of her. "But I believe God has called me here. Some days I don't quite understand it, but this is the next step on my journey. I try hard to be faithful to that call."

Clearly embarrassed at having said so much, she switched back to me. "Green is a nice place to live, Lois. You'll settle in just fine. Just remember that people aren't all that used to newcomers here, and they don't much like change. But God sometimes wants people to change, you know. I see that all the time."

Feeling suddenly antsy, I needed to think about change all right—changing the tire on my car to something more dependable. I thanked her again for her help. "Guess I'd better head back to town. Good luck with your sermon."

"Come on back Sunday at eleven and see what you think," she said.

"Oh, I'm just settling in and not sure when my things are coming. Besides, I'm not much of a churchgoer. I may stop in one of these days. Thanks for asking."

I was not prepared to commit to church on my first Sunday in Green. My plans for the next year didn't include a commitment to anything other than the paper.

When I returned to the newspaper plant, reporter Alex, fresh back from his meeting, brought the news that town leader Major Wilson was peeved with me. "He thought you would show up at the police jury meeting to introduce yourself and get to know everybody."

Come to find out, the car dealer/real estate developer was also on the "po-lice" jury, as Alex called it. The young reporter apologized about mentioning my arrival to Major. "He already knew, though. Said Dub and Chuck told him weeks ago. You know, Miss Lois, he's a big cheese in town and a golfing buddy of the McCullers. You might want to give him a call."

"So any real news from the meeting?" I asked, uncomfortable with this kid giving me advice.

"Well, the huge development on Bayou Lake is moving forward. The jury gave it a unanimous green light, despite complaints from the neighborhood it will affect. They're planning to tear down about a dozen houses, mostly poor people, mostly Blacks—I mean, African Americans—on the lakefront. Build houses on stilts that sort of stick out over the water."

He paused, his investigative lightbulb switching on. "The same kind of house they turned down for Dr. Taylor a few months ago—Kevin Taylor, that is. I need to look into that a little more." He jotted a handful of words into his notebook and stuck his pen behind his ear.

I had covered enough political meetings to know anything can happen, but was puzzled at how this had gotten pushed through. "Won't there be political fallout? What about the commissioners—or police jurors or whatever you call them—from the areas around the development?"

"Major and his friends own the property, and they intend to make a lot of money and develop their own little compound over there. You'll learn soon enough that a handful of people in this town have all the power. What they say goes. Most of those folks have money. The ones who lose don't.

The jurors from that area know which side their bread is buttered on."

Troubled both by what seemed to be the unfairness of the decision and my etiquette faux pas at missing the meeting with Green's movers and shakers, I headed to the phone. I was more worried at that moment about irritating people who paid the paper's bills than I was by the housing development. After all, the guy did own the property. It was his to do with as he wanted. Those people could find other places to live, surely. It was prime real estate, after all, and they were just renters.

A handful of phone calls later, I had set up meet-and-greets with my new challenge, Major Wilson, and with Eva Hillburn, who owned the Ford dealership and Wilson's Department Store. I had also left a message for Mr. Marcus Taylor, head of the Lakeside Neighborhood Association. Starting tomorrow, I would make it a point to see and be seen, getting out and making contacts.

I dialed Marti in the newsroom, but she was running between meetings and couldn't talk.

"Hang in there," she said. It was one of those rushed conversations I recalled well from my city desk days. Next I called the moving company for an update on the arrival of my belongings. Suddenly, sleeping in my own bed was incredibly appealing.

Still restless, I headed to the newsroom and

edited a few stories, trying not to grimace at run-on leads about spaghetti supper fund-raisers and an upcoming revival at the First Baptist Church. I made a few suggestions on headlines and how photographs should be cropped.

A crisis developed when an ad in the second section fell through. "I've got this big hole that needs filling," Tammy said from the composing room. "I can't decide between those reader recipes left over from Tuesday's paper and this filler house ad." She held up copy that reminded people to place a garage sale ad, three lines for three dollars. "Lots of people like their yard sales."

As I wondered how much money the extra newsprint would cost, pressman Stan ambled in to tell me we had a problem with the press, and he needed to drive up to Shreveport to get a part. He thought he could be back by 8 p.m. and have it fixed in time to run the next day's paper and to print the little free-delivery job we did on the side.

"How much is the part?" I asked. "Are you sure the one you've got can't be fixed? What about getting the part locally? What if you don't get back in time? We have to get the paper out, no matter what. What are our options?"

My questions revealed my fear and ignorance.

"Miss Lois," he said. "I've worked on this old press for twenty-five years, and I'll get her up and running in time for tomorrow's paper. Now trust me. Sign this purchase order, and I'll hit the road."

I gulped and signed. It was a good thing I had a free house and a year to figure this out.

6

Adopting a nutria litter for family pets was not a smart idea, according to Wildlife & Fisheries officials who were called to a Bouef Parish home after the animals ran amok, tearing up furniture and terrorizing neighborhood children. "Pets are pets," one agent, who asked not to be identified, said. "Wild animals are wild animals. Quit trying to mix them."

—The Green News-Item

Tammy opened the door for me on Friday morning a bit more cheerfully than she had the day before.

"Doughnuts," I said, pausing to release the latch on the lobby gate. "Celebrating my first edition as owner of *The Green News-Item*." Moving around the building, I had fun holding up the green-and-white paper boxes. "Chocolate? Glazed? Maple?" The latter was my addition to the newspaper's doughnut tradition.

"Thank you for helping get the paper out," I

said, wandering from department to department, learning a little more about these people whose paychecks I now signed. My challenge was to discover who would help me make it in the coming year and who would hold me back. My corporate HR training courses from Dayton would come in handy.

Lee Roy was in his office with the door shut, arguing with someone on the phone, but everyone else was apparently in a fairly decent mood. They treated me with the caution you always treat a new boss, but they didn't seem agitated.

Stan had worked some sort of pressman magic on Bossy. "Don't worry, Miss Lois," he said, taking three doughnuts, one of each. "We'll be right on time this morning if I get the pages from the newsroom."

Wandering over to the composing area, I saw several pages nearly ready to go, with my picture and a big front-page headline reading, "Out-of-state Owner Buys *News-Item*." Also on the page: "Police Jury Okays Houses," "Fine Feathered Friends: Blow Dryer Helps Teen Create Champion Chickens" and "Granny B. Celebrates 100th with Wit and Wisdom."

"Wait," I said to Tammy, scanning the page. "We need to change that head. I'm not an out-of-state owner. I now live in Green." I avoided the champion chicken story and moved on to the birthday article. "And does that story on Granny

B. really go on Page One? Is that the best we have?"

Alex walked up, clearly hands-on in every aspect of the paper at the ripe age of twenty-two. "What do you want the main headline to say?"

"Use bigger type and say, '*News-Item* Sold.'"

"That story on Granny B. is good," he said, a doughnut in his hand. "Have you read it? There are some great quotes, and the woman is a hoot. And that chicken story is interesting. The girl won eight thousand dollars at the Louisiana State Fair last year. She has to wash her chicken with four buckets of water and blow it dry to make it pretty."

I watched Tammy change the main headline, glanced at the feature stories, and mumbled something about letting them stay. Alex was right. We needed good stories about local people.

Two hours later when the presses rolled, I stood by with pride and admired the way the paper looked, all two sections and sixteen pages of it, with a house ad about garage sales and a page full of free weddings and anniversaries. I winced at a long story from a national drug company on improving your sex life, a story obviously copied directly from a press release and plugged in after I'd looked over the pages. I might hear from readers on that one. But the rest of the paper looked good, solid, and real.

"Good feeling, isn't it?" Stan said, as he leafed

through pages. "Never ceases to amaze me when it rolls off."

Standing next to the press as it spit out more copies, I checked each page again. A small thrill ran through me. The part-time photographer even surfaced to take a picture "for the archives," as he put it. I decided to frame those pictures—one of Stan handing me a first edition of *The News-Item* coming off the press and one of me looking through that day's paper.

A tiny group of mostly older people waited out back to deliver their routes, and Iris Jo pulled around in a small purple pickup truck. Climbing out, she introduced me to the motley group of carriers, who welcomed me to town but paid little attention to me.

"What are you doing out here?" I asked Iris. "We shorthanded?"

She smiled. "We're always shorthanded, Miss Lois. But I throw this route for fun—gets me out of the office. I head right out to Route 2 and get in some good visiting every Tuesday and Friday afternoon. Besides, it eases up the load on Stan, and he appreciates that." She nodded toward the pressman/mechanic/delivery guy, who was tossing bundles of papers off the dock to various carriers.

Suddenly, she frowned. "Is that going to be a problem? I mean, do you want me to stay in the office all the time? Do you mind me throwing a route?"

I didn't know what I wanted, needed, or expected. "No problem," I said and turned my attention to Stan, a lean man in his forties. He smiled and chatted quietly with the carriers as he worked.

Watching the process unfold, I was struck by how everyone pitched in. At big-city papers, each person had a specific job. Most people didn't volunteer for anything extra and tried to pass work off to others when possible. Here it was less clear-cut.

Shaking my head, I walked back in and stopped by Alex's desk. "Your story on the new lake development is a good read," I said, shaking his hand. "You put Major Wilson on the spot and got him to admit plans need to be made for displaced tenants. That's good reporting."

His look of pride mirrored that of my reporters in Dayton, and he leaned so far back in his desk chair that I thought he might fall over.

"I'm working on some new information," he said. "I'm poking around to see if I can find out why they turned down Dr. Taylor's house and let these go through. And I heard through the grapevine that some E.P.A. analysis has yet to be done. There could be an impact on water quality." He referred to his notes. "Supposedly, Major's trying to cut that agency out. There have been complaints that he's letting sewage from his houses drain into the lake."

"Good work," I said. "Keep digging. See what you can come up with."

Heading back to my office to prepare for my afternoon meetings, I nearly bumped into Lee Roy.

"Oh, Miss Lois, I was just coming to see you. Wonder if you want me to take you around town this afternoon . . . for your meetings, I mean."

Surprised that he knew I had set up visits with the city leaders, I paused and then decided he might provide insight into these unknown people I was meeting with. "That sounds good. Can you head out now?"

"Sure thing, ma'am," he said. He grabbed his coat and turned off the light in his office.

The afternoon turned out to be interesting and excruciating. The excitement of putting out my first edition subsided, and the reality of small-town politics settled in.

Our first stop was at Major Wilson's real estate office, a modern wood building across the street from the lake, with a nice water view. An attractive woman in her early thirties greeted us and gave Lee Roy a little hug. She looked awkward, as if she didn't know whether to shake my hand, hug me, or do nothing. She took a step back and dropped her hands to her sides. "Welcome to Green, Miss Lois," she said. "I'm Linda."

She ushered us back into Major's office, a large cluttered room with a couple of deer heads and mounted fish—bass, I thought—on the wall.

Major stood up and greeted us enthusiastically, shook hands with Lee Roy, and gave me the weird for-women-only grip. He was in his middle sixties, a bit overweight, and sported a large duck on his brass belt buckle.

"I see you met Linder," he said, putting an "er" on the end of her name. "Can she get you anything? Coffee? Coke?" Without a pause, he looked at his assistant and said, "I'll take a Coke, heavy on the ice."

I declined any refreshments to avoid burping my way through my first visit with a town father. Linda returned with a Coke for Major and a Diet Sprite for Lee Roy, something he apparently drank on a regular basis because he had not even asked for it.

"Thank you so much for taking time to meet with me, sir," I said.

Major interrupted before I could say how happy I was to be in Green. "Sir? Let's get rid of that sir business. I ain't that old."

He laughed as he said it, as though it were super funny. "Call me Major. We're glad to have you down here in Louisiana. Where is that you're from again? Illinois? Or was it Michigan?" He didn't pause, and I realized he didn't care where I was from. "I met that friend of yours—the one who bought the paper. Seemed like a nice enough fellow. Sorry about your loss. What you think about our little community?"

I waited to answer, not sure if he would interrupt me again. "Speak up, girl," he said, shocking me with his arrogance.

"Green's a nice place," I said. "I look forward to getting to know more about it and the people here."

"What are your plans?" he asked. "You heading out in a few days?"

The question startled me, and I glanced at Lee Roy, who watched intently for my response.

Suddenly it hit me. Lee Roy expected me to leave town and let him run the paper. He planned on it. Major Wilson knew and expected it too.

"Oh no," I said. "I've moved to Green. I'll be here for quite a while. I'm eager to work with you and help with your advertising needs. I want to do what I can for Bouef Parish."

Lee Roy made a choking sound and set down his Sprite. "Went down the wrong way," he said. He pulled out his handkerchief, wiped his mouth, and then blotted a spill on his pristine shirt.

The next hour passed slowly, with me on the edge of the leather wingback I had chosen and Lee Roy slumped on the end of an overstuffed couch.

"Bouef Parish is a fine place to call home," Major said, "but it isn't the easiest place to do business, or to be in politics, for that matter. You can't please some people. They'll tell you they want things to be different but then tell you they don't like change. They don't get how tough it is to move things forward."

"You do a good job," Lee Roy jumped in. "You've worked wonders in this town. You turned the real estate market around and got us that highway. Didn't let yourself be railroaded by those naysayers. You got that paper mill to come here too."

Suddenly Lee Roy turned toward me. "Make sure you don't get in his way. Major makes things happen. He is a true patriot too. A fine fellow." His speech sounded like he was trying to sell me on a potential blind-date candidate.

"We get it done, don't we, Roy?" Major asked, winking as he said it.

I had digested about all of Major that I could. "We better be going. We've got another stop to make today," I said. "I can't wait to watch you in action, Major. Learn how it's done." I was not above sucking up to this guy if it made my life easier.

"Linder," Major yelled suddenly. "Get Miss Lois here one of our coffee mugs and a calendar."

"Yes, sir," she said, hopping up so quickly her chair rolled back and hit the fax machine. She scrambled over to a metal cabinet and pulled the items out. It had been awhile since I had seen someone move that quickly to follow a boss's order. "Here you go, ma'am."

"It's Lois, Linda. Thanks. I look forward to seeing you again. Maybe I could buy you lunch one day."

As Lee Roy and I got in the car, I had to ask. "What's his story?"

My ad director, circulation manager, and apparently owner-wannabe shrugged, as though deciding if he could be bothered to answer.

"The usual. Major's an important guy in town—a power broker. You know he owns the Chevy dealership out on the edge of town and he's got his real estate business. He developed some real nice subdivisions for Green. Helps the area, helps the paper. He ran for office about a dozen years ago and decided he likes that too. Does everything and is a heckuva golfer. Been friends with the McCullers for years."

He stopped, pursed his lips, and looked as though he didn't know if he had said too little or too much. I wanted to know more, especially about Lee Roy's relationship with Major, but at this point I didn't want to be too obvious.

"Is that his real name?"

"His real name's Bill, but he's gone by Major since his days in the Army Reserve right after college." That was all Lee Roy was going to say about Major.

We parked on the street near the side entrance of Wilson's Department Store and headed in for our meeting with Eva Hillburn. After Major, I didn't know what to expect. We walked directly into the office, skirting an empty desk out front.

"Louise takes Friday afternoons off," Lee Roy said as we passed. "Let's go on back."

Eva was on the phone when we entered, but waved us to sit down. She was a tiny woman in her mid- to late-fifties, with a helmet of dyed black hair—hair so black that it looked like the color would rub off on your hand. Intricately poufed—yes, pouf is the only word I could think of—it didn't seem to be so much a hairstyle as an arrangement. I wondered what was in there.

I tried to take my eyes and mind off her hair and focus on the office and the rest of the woman. I finally had to make myself look away. Her desk was a small, ornately carved, dark wood antique. An Asian screen with hand-painted cranes sat in the corner. Some sort of silk-looking cloth behind glass hung nearby. Other Far Eastern pieces dotted the room, including a handful of vases and a few interesting mementoes. Everything was spotless, without a hint of clutter. Even her desk was nearly empty.

I judged and dismissed Eva as someone who had inherited money, didn't do any real work, and probably went to the beauty parlor and the country club on the same day every week.

How wrong I was. Her phone conversation blew that theory.

As I settled into my chair, she continued a complicated discussion about an upcoming meeting in Europe. "We have a major problem in Budapest," she said in a professional tone and then proceeded to outline a half-dozen things that needed to be done right away.

I realized the knick-knacks that decorated her office were souvenirs of world business travels, not something she had picked up at Pier One.

"Great. I'll check back with you on Monday. Keep me posted from your end."

Hanging up the phone, she walked around the desk to give my hand a firm shake, nodding to Lee Roy in the process. "I apologize for keeping you waiting. Good to meet you, Lois. Happy to have you in Green. Nice to get some new blood in town."

"My pleasure," I said. "It's an interesting place. So you've lived here awhile?"

"Born and raised. Went off to college and followed my ex-husband to West Texas but came to my senses and headed home. I love this community, even if it does wear on you at times."

My "go-to guy" sat on the edge of his chair, noticeably less at home here than he had been at Major's. He frowned at Eva's last comment.

"What are your plans for *The News-Item*? Any changes in store there?" Eva asked.

"I hope to build on the traditions of the paper and do what's needed to take things to the next level. I'll assess the situation before I jump in." My voice had the personality of a bowl of Jell-O without any fruit in it. Eva Hillburn looked at me in a way that told me she knew I was feeding her a line of bull.

"We can use some change around here," she said. "I hope you'll be a leader in that direction."

"I hope so too," I said, although I didn't see myself being much of a leader in this dumpy town.

"I'm sure you know that Wilson's Department Store and Hillburn's Ford are big advertisers," Eva said. I winced, waiting for her to make some demand I didn't want to hear. "I look forward to working with you and continuing our good relationship."

"I look forward to that too," I said, "as does Lee Roy." The ad director looked surprised when I mentioned his name.

"We've hit some snags in the past, as I'm sure Lee Roy has told you," Eva said, "and I don't want that to get in the way of moving ahead."

My go-to guy had mentioned nothing about snags, bumps, or any other problems.

"We worked that out, Ms. Hillburn, as you know." He cleared his throat. "That was a silly misunderstanding."

"I suppose it was," she said.

Lee Roy looked at his watch and stood up abruptly. "We need to be getting back to the paper, Lois."

He walked out ahead of me, and I reached out to shake Eva's hand again. She looked me right in the eye and smiled. "It's good to have another woman business owner in town. I can't wait to see what you do."

"I'll need your advice along the way," I said. "I'd appreciate any help you can give me."

When we got in the car, I turned to Lee Roy.

"Snags? What snags? Anything the owner might need to know?" I did not like being caught off guard. Plus, Lee Roy's chumminess with Major had gotten on my nerves more than I wanted to say.

"Sorry," he mumbled, driving back to the paper. "Ms. Hillburn got a bit perturbed over some advertising rates and a story we didn't follow up on. She pulled her ads for a month. That hurt. We had to go over there and beg her to get them back, me and Dub and Chuck. It was tricky. But she needs us as much as we need her, so I knew she would come back."

I interrupted. "What was the story she was interested in?"

He rolled his head around on his shoulders, the way you do when your neck feels tight. "She was upset that we didn't run a story on some problems with pollution in the lake and some concerns raised about Mossy Bend." Mossy Bend was Major's first big development on the north end of the lake, a gated community of expensive houses owned by local people with money and out-of-towners who wanted a getaway home.

Lee Roy did not continue. I felt the way I had once in a newspaper deposition, where I was instructed to briefly answer the question asked, nothing more. He seemed to have been to the same school of information coaching.

"And the advertising issue?" I asked.

"She was upset, yeah, upset would be the right word, with some rates she was getting."

"Why? What sort of rates?"

Now he rolled his shoulders, too, as though the muscle pain was more intense and moving down his body. "She thought we were giving her brother a better rate."

"Her brother?"

"Yeah, Major. You know, he's her brother."

I had not known, and I was even more annoyed that Lee Roy hadn't dropped that fact on me earlier. Now that I thought about it, Eva Hillburn did run Wilson's Department Store, and Wilson was Major's last name. I should have picked up on that. I needed to learn quickly who was related to whom, who was divorced from whom, and who had an axe to grind.

Instead of focusing on the omission of key information, I went right to the money/advertising issue. "And were we giving her brother a better price?"

Pulling into the newspaper lot, Lee Roy parked and looked at me. "Yes, we were. He's a bigger player, had more linage, so we went off the rate card for him. That development cost him a lot of money, and we wanted to help him out, help the town. I thought we were overcharging him. Dub and Chuck agreed. It was none of Eva's business, but she's still mad that Major tried to sell the family store out from under her."

I was ready to call it a day and get out of the car with Lee Roy. I was nearly dizzy, wondering who I could trust and what my role would be in dealing with this cast of characters.

Everything was so unfamiliar.

I didn't like not knowing what I was doing.

7

The nearby community of Lake Village has joined municipal governments nationwide in approving an ordinance banning sagging pants on men and women in public. Councilwoman Lucinda Lovelady authored the ordinance, calling the display of underwear "outrageous and an affront to dignity everywhere, and it doesn't matter if they're Hanes or Wal-Mart brand."

—The Green News-Item

A tall African American woman sat behind the counter in the Lakeside Motel office, reading a Bible. She didn't notice me until I said, "Excuse me," and then she jumped and shrieked. "Oh, child, you scared me! I didn't hear you come in. May I help you?"

The woman was stately. She was dressed nicely in a casual shirt and skirt and wore glasses that she took off as we spoke and let dangle around her neck by a chain. I introduced myself and asked to extend my reservation. "I also wanted to let you know how much I have enjoyed my stay so far," I said. "I hope you will let the owners know how much I appreciate the room."

"I expect I can do that," she said with a smile and held out her hand. "I'm Pearl Taylor. My husband and I own the Lakeside. I think you left a message for my husband, by the way. He's the head of the Lakeside Neighborhood Association."

I was mortified. I assumed she was hired help. I knew from reporter Alex that her husband was an influential man in town, one I needed to get to know. I stammered and told Mrs. Taylor I was happy to meet her and looked forward to hearing from Mr. Taylor and practically ran backward out of the room.

"Monday week," she said as I was leaving. "He hopes to meet with you Monday week about five o'clock. Will that work? Maybe you could stay for supper?"

I stopped. "Monday week? This coming Monday?"

"Next Monday," she said. "The week after this coming week."

"That's a new one for me." I tried to stop myself from frowning.

"I believe I have bumfuzzled you," she said with a laugh. "But I do hope you'll come anyway. Not this Monday but the next."

"I'd love to come. Thank you." I accidentally spun gravel while leaving the parking lot. Bumfuzzled? Monday week? With everything else I had to keep up with, I clearly needed a lesson in talking Southern.

Downtown on a weekend was as deserted as it had been on New Year's Day, with the exception of a couple of pickups and minivans at the antique mall. *The News-Item* building was eerily empty. I roamed through each department, trying to get a better sense of the place. This reeked of snooping, but I considered it the new owner's prerogative.

In the advertising-marketing area, a huge ivy sat on a filing cabinet with a big sign that said, "Do Not Water This Plant." I tried to imagine stealth employees coming in and secretly watering the plant. The same person who made "Flush after Using" signs for the women's bathroom probably wrote this sign. Or maybe it was the person who had changed the bathroom signs to read, "Blush after Using."

The news area was the most interesting, of course. If journalists put the same creativity into the paper as they did into their cubicles, newspapers would be in much better shape. Horror action figures and funky postcards of oversized mail-boxes and rocking chairs and a giant pickle on a train covered Alex's desk. The work area next to his was covered with stacks of books and oddities, including what looked to be the entire cast of *Star Wars* made out of Peeps, those bright colored marshmallows you get at Easter. Baffled, I sat down at the desk to study this bizarre work of art.

"Like my sculptures?" a deep voice asked close to my ear.

I gasped at a high-pitched inhuman sound. When I turned around, a frumpy old guy who needed a shave stood within six inches of me. He was wearing a green eyeshade, the kind news-paper editors wore in the old days. His clothes were wrinkled with bits of dried food on them. His sweatshirt said, "Nothing goes right when your underwear's tight."

He held out his hand. "Tom McNutt, weekend cops reporter, copy editor, and classified adver-tising layout person. You must be the new owner."

I stood up, slowly took his hand, wishing it were just a bit cleaner and feeling guilty he had caught me at his desk. "Tom? Hernia surgery, right?"

He nodded, and we exchanged the usual pleas-antries about how he was feeling.

"You did this?" I asked, pointing to his desk.

"Yep. I have the entire cast of *Lord of the Rings* at home. You know Peeps are not as easy to work with as you might think, but they were ninety percent off at the Dollar Hut, so the price was right."

"I imagine so," I said and backed away from him a few feet. I was uneasy in the room alone with him, but surely he wasn't a mass murderer. He worked for me, for heaven's sake.

"I just made a pot of coffee," he said, pointing toward the break area near the composing room. "Want a cup?"

The next few minutes we dug around for a clean cup and made small talk. I have never understood how offices get the collection of coffee mugs they do and how they become so hopelessly filthy. The only thing worse than the coffee area would be the refrigerator, I was certain.

Tom had worked at the paper for an amazing thirty-nine years, starting as a copy boy back when it was a daily and doing every imaginable job since.

"See this scar," he said, holding out his hand. "Accidentally slammed my hand onto one of those spikes where the newspaper copy used to be put. Remember those?" I winced and nodded, then decided this was better than seeing his hernia scar.

"I have diabetes. That's why I wear these," he said, holding up a foot covered with a black boot. "And high blood pressure. I would have loved to have become a full-time reporter when I was a young'un, but I didn't have the gumption for it."

He briefly interrupted his life story. "What color sugar you want?" he asked. "Pink or yellow?"

I turned down his sweetener offer. I was a black coffee kind of woman. Tom, however, must like his sweet because he tore open four packets and poured them in the cup, followed by a liberal shaking of lumpy creamer. "Nectar of the gods," he said as he took his first sip.

"Well, I was just exploring the building a little bit," I said. "Guess I'll head on back to my office."

"Good luck to you," he said. "Let me know what I can do you for."

I walked purposefully toward my office, acting as though I had important business to take care of. Unlocking my door, I sat down in the fake leather desk chair that was way too big for me. In my mind's eye, I looked like Edith Ann—that Lily Tomlin character—little person, huge chair.

An attempt to call Marti proved fruitless. She was probably getting her nails done or out for her Saturday morning long run.

I went into the conference room to sort through some boxes the Big Boys had left, pulling out a ragged file that said "History." Tom had surprised me when he said he had worked at the paper when it was a daily, so I settled in to read a lengthy history of *The News-Item*, on yellow, brittle paper.

The story was fascinating, written by Helen McCuller, sister to the father of the Big Boys and matriarch of the family. The narrative was more intriguing since I would be living in the author's house on Route 2.

Helen told how the paper had been a fiery daily, with a reputation for getting wrongs righted. "Governors and senators and important businessmen came to call on the newspaper, needing its support for their causes," she wrote. "*The News-Item* was one of the first voices to suggest that cotton would not always be king and that Blacks had the right to vote." Both stances had gotten the front windows broken and the presses sabotaged.

Slowly the area changed. Agriculture lost much of its sway. The parish was heavily integrated. Many people moved to Shreveport or Dallas, looking for better jobs and more money. Television and air-conditioning came along and sent people indoors. The interstate bypassed the town, cutting down on the little commerce that flowed through the area. The community shrank, and *The News-Item* shrank right along with it.

What had Ed been thinking? How was I going to keep us going for a year and find a buyer?

I retreated to the to-do list in my notebook, determined to set up an appointment with the bank on Monday and to find a pest guy to get rid of the rats at the house. I fished around for an index card with some phone numbers that Iris Jo had given me. She laughingly called it my new BlackBerry.

"Iris Jo, this is Lois Barker," I said on the phone. "Am I calling at a bad time?"

"Heavens no." She sounded pleased to hear my

voice. "I was just vacuuming. How's your first Saturday in Green?"

"Oh, it's going fine," I said. "I'm up at the office getting organized. I wondered if you could recommend someone to exterminate rats?"

"Sure. Terry Bradshaw," she said.

"Terry Bradshaw? Like the quarterback?"

"No relation," she said, "but he's your man. Might want him to spray for roaches while he's out there. He goes to my church, good advertiser, too. Let me see if I can run him down for you."

This was my lesson in how business was done at the newspaper in Green. Somebody knew somebody, usually through church or a relative. That somebody often was a good advertiser or might become an advertiser. I seldom made my own calls for any kind of service work.

Tackling another set of files, I dug out an ancient calculator, the kind that made a sort of grinding noise when you hit the equal button. Profits had definitely spiraled downward after Ed bought the paper. I had a challenge ahead of me, but I wasn't up to it today.

I stuck my head in the news area and waved goodbye to Tom, who saluted me and went back to a game of solitaire on his computer. The police radio blared as usual, but things were quiet otherwise.

As I walked out of the building, I noticed the death notices had been updated—painted by Tom,

I supposed—and the smoking teenager sat on the steps over by the dock, where she had been the day I pulled into town. Doing a slight turn, I walked over and said "hello," in a voice that sounded a little snippy, even to me.

"I'm Lois Barker, the new owner of *The News-Item*. I noticed you out here the other day. Can I help you with something? Are you waiting for someone?"

The girl was about sixteen and very cute, in a funky sort of way. Her red hair was longer in the front, with interesting blondish layering in the back. I knew from water-cooler discussions in Dayton that those lowlights were not easy to pull off. She had on tight jeans, a pink velvet coat with fake fur trim and some boots I had seen on an actress in *People* magazine recently.

She stared at me for about thirty seconds, with that go-away-and-leave-me-alone look. Then she stood up and walked slowly away. "Nope. Don't need anything. Not waiting for anyone."

She stopped briefly, as if to say something. Instead, she tossed down her cigarette, ground it out, dug around in a big hobo style purse, pulled out a bright green lighter, lit another cigarette, and kept on walking.

I got in my car and took a drive out to Route 2, homesick for Dayton and my life there. Halfway to the new place, I did a U-turn and spent the next two hours walking up and down every aisle in

Wal-Mart, buying a few things I needed and a bunch of things I didn't.

As I drove back to the motel, I saw the girl in the pink coat walking through the run-down neighborhood across the street, smoking yet another cigarette.

8

Green Middle School student Suzanne Seal will be lunching with the governor in November. Suzanne, 13, daughter of Jack and Cindy Seal, Route 2, won the Northwest Louisiana Art in the Schools Award with a watercolor of her nine-year-old sister, Gracie.

—The Green News-Item

Perhaps Green residents could have chosen a more central location to build a tribute to the boll weevil.

Winding around back roads for more than an hour, I searched for the local landmark, a monument to the insect that destroyed cotton crops. The jaunt seemed like a good way to kill a Sunday morning—until I became hopelessly lost.

Heading out of town on an unfamiliar highway, I turned right here, left there, and was soon on a gravel road. Completely lost, I noticed a man working around some ponds and headed toward him, walking carefully across a muddy path so as to avoid any snakes and ruining my new shoes. Three barking dogs charged at me, but the man called them back, and they calmed down.

"Excuse me," I said, "but I think I'm lost. Can you tell me how to get back to Green?"

He brushed his muddy hands off on his jeans, ran one hand through his hair and said, "You are turned around, aren't you?" By now the hounds were running back up to me, and he called them again. "Mannix. Markey. Kramer. Get back over here . . . now!"

Before I could ponder the names of the barking trio, Mr. Pond Man walked up and gestured as he talked. "Turn right here and head back up the main highway. You'll pass a little crossroads with a store. There'll be a handful of houses, more cat-fish ponds and then a church on your right. Go right, and you'll head straight into town."

"Oh, so these are catfish ponds," I said, almost to myself.

"Yes, ma'am, they sure are." I was talking to my first ever catfish farmer. "I'm Chris Craig. Are you visiting someone in Green?"

"No, I just moved here. I'm Lois Barker. Good to meet you." Feeling ridiculously out of place, I turned back toward my car. "Thanks for the directions. Good luck with your fish."

The crossroads appeared quickly. The Jot 'Em

Down Grocery's hand-lettered sign read: "Hardware, Plate Lunches, Bait." The store's hours sign said, "Monday–Saturday, 11:30 Till It's Gone," and I wondered if that meant the plate lunches or the bait. A note on the door said, "Closed Sundays for Church. God's Service Is Better Than Ours."

Pulling away from the store, I saw the monument and laughed out loud. There, at the crossroads, across from the hardware, lunch, and bait store was a majestic marble statue with a Greek goddess figure holding her arms straight out with a giant bug in her hands. This was a "copy of a figure someone had seen while visiting kinfolks in Alabama," according to Aunt Helen's history of the paper. "Green residents built it as a thank you to the insect for forcing us to quit being so dependent on cotton."

I got out, took a picture on my cell phone, and sent it to Marti with a message that said, "Welcome to my world."

Apparently, this was the main street of an old community, with a monument to a boll weevil, a grocery store that sold night crawlers and home cooking, one house, and a dilapidated church that was so overgrown, even in winter, you could hardly see it.

After about a quarter of a mile, though, things began to look familiar. I was on Route 2, right in front of the house I was scheduled to move into if my furniture ever arrived. I turned into the driveway and sat for a few minutes. It only looked slightly better today than I remembered. The porch and roof had some interesting lines, details I had not noticed before, but the yard was huge and needed work.

Oh well. I could live anywhere for a year.

Backing out, not expecting anyone for miles, I nearly ran into an old pickup, driven by the guy from the ponds. He waved. I waved back and fell in behind him until he turned into the mobile home near the church. So those were the dogs Iris Jo used in her directions to my house.

A trickle of cars pulled into the little Grace Community Chapel parking lot, and I realized it was fifteen minutes till church started. I turned at the sign that said, "Exercise daily. Walk with the Lord." Admittedly, I would have done just about anything to avoid going back to that motel or to the newspaper.

As soon as I pulled in, I nearly turned around and pulled out. I wasn't dressed for church. I didn't go to church. I didn't want to talk to these people. I knew what would happen if I walked in. They would see a visitor, and they would pounce, sort of like fresh meat to a lion on the prowl. Before it was over, I'd be invited to a potluck lunch, and they'd try to sign me up for a committee.

As I put the car in reverse, a smiling woman

made eye contact and waved. It was Iris Jo. "Hey, Lois, good to have you here," she said. "I didn't expect to see you today."

Like it or not, I was going in.

My employee wore church clothes with a nice navy blue jacket. I had on wrinkled khakis and a wool sweater with a canvas green coat. While I was generally happy with my tall, slender appearance, my sense of style lacked something today. Even my cute casual shoes were caked with mud.

"Well, I was just out exploring and decided to stop in. Pastor Jean helped me with my flat the other day and invited me. I thought it might be good to get to know some people in the community."

That had not been my intention at all, but now that I was here, I might as well make it look like I had planned it. "I hope it's okay that I'm wearing casual clothes."

I gestured at my sloppy gear, and Iris Jo dismissed my concern immediately.

"Not a problem," she said. "We're a casual country church. No dress code. You can even wear flip-flops in the summer. Look, I've got to run. I sing in the choir, and we usually have a quick practice. Just make yourself at home." She turned around, smiling again. "You don't sing, do you?"

"Good grief, no," I said. "I have not an ounce of singing talent." I was not being falsely modest.

"Oh, well, make a joyful noise," she said, and

off she went, animated in a way I had not noticed in our few encounters at the paper. She struck me as a quiet woman, almost pensive, much of the time.

I stood out like a sore thumb at Grace Community.

No matter what Iris Jo said, people did dress up for church, at least in skirts or nice slacks. A few of the older women had on dresses. Most of the men wore ties.

The service opened with a talkative prayer request session, including updates on members who apparently had been absent for a while. "Does anyone know how Herman is?" Pastor Jean asked. A man in work pants and a white shirt raised his hand and said, "They did that defibrillator thing Monday. I think he's home now." From Herman they moved to an update on Samantha, a thirteen-month-old with cancer, and a quick report on Althea's boys who both were in the military in the Middle East.

"I've got a praise report," another woman said. "My Daddy's doing much better since they found out he was doubling up on his pain medication. He'll be able to go back to the nursing home this coming week." Folks nodded and said, "Praise God" and things like that, surprising me somewhat. They seemed a pretty somber bunch.

"Katy, good to see you back with us today," Pastor Jean said, with a warm smile, and I was shocked to see she was talking to the girl in the pink coat with the fake fur trim. The girl had her arms wrapped tight around her. She did not respond to the pastor's comments, staring right at her, and a middle-aged woman next to her patted her on the shoulder.

I don't know why her presence surprised me. I guess that I generally didn't think of cigarette-smoking teenagers as churchgoers. And Pastor Jean had welcomed her back. I wonder where she had been? Living with her dad maybe? Off at a drug rehab center?

I began the game of trying to figure out the situation with scarcely any information, but finally gave up and decided to ask Iris Jo.

From prayer time, we moved into a brief welcome and announcements session. I knew my presence would not go uncommented upon. "Anyone have any guests today?" Jean asked, and Iris Jo stood up. "I'm happy to introduce Miss Lois Barker, soon to be our neighbor on Route 2 and new owner of *The Green News-Item*."

"Stand up, Miss Lois," someone down the pew said. I obediently rose and did a wave, sort of like you might do in a convertible during a parade.

Pastor Jean looked a bit surprised and smiled. "Welcome, Lois. I didn't know you'd be here today. Good to see you."

People clapped, and so I was introduced to Green's faithful, or at least this little flock of them.

The congregation was very small. I counted thirty-four worshippers, plus the nine people in the choir. A middle-aged woman playing the piano was also the choir director, and one time she got started on the wrong hymn and laughed and started over. "Sorry, I thought we were doing another song." She did not seem to take things too seriously. This same woman told the congregation, "Now it's a new year, and I want every one of you to sing a solo this year. I mean everybody. Just see me after church." People said "amen" like they thought it was a good idea.

Pastor Jean wore a pair of dangly earrings that kept bumping her little microphone, making a thump every time she moved her head, but she didn't appear to notice. She read the passage from the book of James she had mentioned to me the day I had the flat, and then said a quick prayer. "Dear God, please give me wisdom to lead your church and to speak your words. Use me to do Thy work, and forgive me for the many ways in which I fall short."

My mind drifted as she spoke, and I began to write a new to-do list for the week ahead on my bulletin, looking up occasionally as though I took notes on the sermon. I noticed the man who had reported on the ill Herman dozed, a couple of small children made squealing noises, and a baby cried. I wasn't sure how Jean kept her mind on her message, but she did—at times seeming to look me right in the eye. "You are not here by accident today," she said. "God has a plan and purpose for your life. People are so afraid of failing, but if God wants you to do something, you don't have to worry about failing because God gets results. He gives you wisdom to do what he wants you to do. If results don't come, you don't have to feel bad about it."

The winter light came through the little church's stained glass windows, and the red cushion made the seat passably comfortable. I did not fall asleep, but I did relax. I even jotted down a few of her comments. When the offering plate came by, I put a twenty-dollar bill in, figuring I owed that for getting my flat fixed.

As I expected, several people came up to talk to me after the service. "Glad to have you today. Hope you'll come back," an elderly man said. "We'd love to have you at our women's Bible study on Thursday," a middle-aged woman said. "Come back for our prayer service on Wednesdays," another lady added.

Iris Jo was among the first, asking me if I wanted to have lunch with her and some friends. I thanked everyone for their kindness and politely declined the invitations.

I walked out and noticed a somewhat familiar face, a good-looking man, one of the few people younger than sixty, giving Iris Jo a big hug. It took a couple of seconds till it hit me that it was catfish farmer/dog man, all cleaned up with a tie on. He must have slipped in after me. He caught me looking at him and smiled, gave a half wave, and went back to his conversation with Iris Jo.

Unable to face another fast-food hamburger, I ate a banana and microwave popcorn in my room before heading to the office. Somehow going in to work made me feel less at loose ends, and the empty building didn't seem quite as creepy as it had the day before. I did a quick check of the break room to make sure Tom wasn't napping on the sofa, waiting to scare me out of my wits. All was clear.

My afternoon consisted of going over the payroll, trying to put a face to every name, and looking over our accounts payable from the last year. Many of the expenditures were ridiculously small, like Alex's $2.25 parking voucher from covering a trial to Tammy's $4.48 reimbursement for tape and Tylenol. Lee Roy was definitely the big spender, with several fairly high-dollar meals, at least by what I had seen of Green meals, and a monthly reimbursement for his country club membership. Oddly, there were no expenses for the Big Boys. They must have taken their money from another account or didn't file expenses.

In the middle of the afternoon, I needed some air. Just as I opened the newspaper's door, the girl in the pink coat walked by, glancing up at me and moving on without a second look.

"Wait!" I yelled, not sure why. "You're Katy, right? How you doing today?"

The girl stood there looking at me as though trying to decide if I were a child molester or a worm.

"I'm Lois," I said. "Lois Barker."

"Yeah, you told me that yesterday."

"I saw you at church today," I said, grasping for anything that might move this conversation along. I was curious about this girl. She had a look in her eyes that reminded me of me when I was her age, a little lost, a little feisty.

"Yeah, so what?" she asked in the surly tone of voice only a teenage girl can master. "My Mother made me go."

"Moms are like that," I said, trying to sound like a co-conspirator. "They think things like church are important for kids. My Mom did that, too."

"Well, I had quit going to church and was getting away with it till . . . well, till my stepdad caught me smoking. Now I have to go every week or I am grounded, can't use my phone and don't get any money."

Suddenly she seemed to realize she was talking about herself to me, and she stopped. But she didn't walk away. Instead, she pointed at the paper. "So you own this place now, huh? That's weird."

"Yeah, it is weird." On that point I could not disagree with her. "My friend got sick and died and left it to me in his will. Isn't that strange? So I have a year to get it all fixed up and sell it."

I couldn't believe I had just said those words. "I mean if I decide to sell it."

"I'm going to beauty school in a year or so," she said. "My mother and stepfather say if I stay in school and make good grades, when I turn eighteen I can quit and get my hair license. I mean I won't be eighteen in a year, but I'll be close, and I bet they'll let me."

"You have a great sense of style," I said, as though I were the editor of *Glamour* or *Cosmo Girl*. "You wear great clothes. You put things together I would never think about. But you do need to give up those cigarettes. They'll kill you. They helped kill my friend."

I had gone from chummy friend to lecturer in a couple of sentences. Her face shifted immediately. "Whatever," she said. "I've got to go."

As she walked off, she turned around and gave a very small wave.

"My friend died, too," she said, and kept walking.

9

My furniture arrived unexpectedly, a week later than planned and a day earlier than expected. I was in the middle of trying to salvage the next day's edition when the call came. I might have freaked out just a smidge.

Advertising linage looked good for the day, but the news report was skimpy. Without any Monday government meetings, we had little meat for the next day's paper and no plan to put any on the table. Alex's follow-up story on the lake development still had not panned out. We had a pretty decent police story about more than a hundred dachshunds being rescued from a house outside Green, along with eleven cats and an iguana, but we hadn't gone much beyond the police report.

There was a nice food package by Anna Grace Adams. "I discovered the newspaper and the First Amendment in my seventies," she told me when I first saw her in the lobby. "Now I'm your food columnist. I wish you'd put me on Page One." Her story this issue was about ways to beat the winter doldrums in the kitchen and included a long batch of reader recipes.

"I'm sorry I don't have more news today," Alex said. His apology surprised me. "I'll do better with upcoming editions. I'm really going somewhere with this zoning story."

Just then Tom meandered by, eating a cookie. "Anyone mentioned the mayor's retiring?" he asked, clearly shocking Alex with the scoop.

At age 92, Mayor Oscar Myers, and that was indeed his name, had decided he had had enough. This was a big story, not only for Green, but the entire state. Myers was the oldest mayor in Louisiana and had been mayor in Green for nearly six decades. Tom picked up the tidbit over at the Cotton Boll Café. "I saw him there and asked him myself, and he said yes."

As I hurried out the door to meet the movers, Alex jumped into high gear and started trying to find the mayor. Tom would look for our one photographer and scour the newsroom's morgue for old photos. "We must have this story," I said, wishing the movers had kept with their schedule as planned. "I'll be back as soon as I can."

By the time I got to the house, the moving van was backed up to the front door and the guys had furniture sitting around the yard, waiting for me to get there. It looked like a giant yard sale with all my favorite stuff. They seemed relieved that there were not any stairs inside, especially when they pulled out my old upright piano. I'm going to learn to play one of these days. I bought this great instrument at an auction in Indiana, and I couldn't bear to part with it. Now, watching these two beefy guys strain as they rolled it up on the porch, I wondered if I should have sold it.

The house had a sort of pesticide smell, and Terry Bradshaw's card lay on the kitchen counter. He had written, "Call me if you need me. I think it's all taken care of." I opened a few cabinets and closets, looking for rats, but didn't see any, dead or alive.

It was nearly 4:30 p.m. when they finished. I needed to get back to the paper and see how the story on the mayor was coming. We could work on it this evening and have it ready to roll in the morning, putting together a package that would do *The News-Item* proud. I turned out the lights and locked up.

Just then I remembered I had an appointment at the Taylor house at five o'clock. I couldn't believe I had forgotten. I didn't have time to go to dinner somewhere. I had work to do. And when was I going to unpack?

I raced back to the paper and stuck my head into the newsroom for a quick update. "I had a great interview with the mayor," Alex said. "Things are coming together. This is going to sell a lot of papers."

"Thanks," I said, on the run and feeling like I was back in Dayton. "I'll edit it later on tonight. Make it good!" I hurried by Iris Jo's desk to ask directions to the Taylor home and to tell her thanks again for getting the bug guy out.

"My pleasure," she said, as though she meant it.

At five minutes after five, I pulled into the Taylor driveway, one of those neat, modest homes right on the lake, near the motel they owned. The sun was setting, leaving a beautiful glow on the horizon, but I didn't have time to appreciate the view.

"I'm sorry I'm late." I began apologizing from the moment Mr. Taylor walked to the door, before I said "hello" or introduced myself. I had spent so many years rushing around that this came as second nature to me, the rapid pulse, thinking up excuses for being late, trying to collect my thoughts on the fly.

"Oh, no problem, no problem at all. Come on in here where it's warm. I'm Marcus Taylor. Welcome to Green."

"Mr. Taylor, I'm Lois Barker. It's a pleasure to

meet you. Thank you so much for having me over this evening."

Pearl Taylor walked in from the back of the house and gave me a small hug, something I was learning people down here in North Louisiana liked to do. "Good to see you again, Miss Lois. Have a seat."

The house was incredibly homey. Compared to the house where my furniture now sat out on Route 2, it looked like heaven. Nothing was fancy, but it all seemed so cozy. There were similarities between the way the Lakeside Motel looked and this home. I sat on the end of an Early American style couch, and Mrs. Taylor sat on the other end. Mr. Taylor sat in an upholstered recliner that clearly was his regular seat. I got the idea that no one sat in the chair except Mr. Taylor.

Pearl wore brown knit slacks and a brown and peach shirt. Marcus had on navy blue slacks and a nice plaid long-sleeved shirt. He was about sixty with graying hair and a quick smile. I had guessed Pearl to be in her late fifties when I encountered her at the motel, and her appearance today confirmed that. Her hair was a deep brown, and she wore it swept up in the back, almost in a French twist.

"We thought we could visit for a while about the neighborhood association and then eat some supper," Mr. Taylor said.

"We invited our daughter for supper, too," Mrs.

Taylor said. "Thought you might enjoy some younger company. And we'd like her to meet you. We hope that's okay."

"Oh, certainly. That's great," I said, alternating between thinking I needed to get back to the paper and it was very nice of them to have me in their home for a meal, the first people in Green to do so.

Our meeting for the next hour and a half was informative and helped put into context a lot that was going on in Green. Sometimes the couple chatted, and at other times Mr. Taylor referred to a handwritten page in a spiral notebook, stressing that he wanted to make sure he covered all his points. I could tell he was taking our conversation very seriously.

Every now and then, his wife got up and went to the kitchen "to check on our supper." Something smelled quite good, and my stomach started to growl.

The couple had been involved in the Lakeside Neighborhood Association for nearly three decades, had helped found it when such community groups sprang up at the grassroots level everywhere. I was surprised when I found out the organization included these homes on the lake and those across the road, the rundown neighborhood known as Lakeside Annex.

"We've lived in this house on the lake for thirty-seven years. Hard to believe," Mr. Taylor said.

"We've owned the motel for nearly twenty-five. My bride here is a retired schoolteacher, and I retired from the post office. I drive a school bus these days, keep those young rowdies in line."

Looking at his notes, he switched gears and made a little statement. "Our association wants to make sure each neighbor is treated fairly, and this precious resource of our lake is never taken for granted. And we want to make the Lakeside Annex a better place to live, upgrade the houses, and hold landlords to property standards. With all of that in mind, we have officially opposed the Cypress Point subdivision, which would limit access to the lake, further pollute the area, and change the texture of our community."

Pearl jumped in. "We bought our home from the Wilson family long before anyone ever thought the property was worth anything. Even though it's on the water, it sits lower than lots of local land. It's a bit swampy in the summertime."

"Most black folks couldn't afford to buy a house back then," Marcus said, "but my Pearl was good with money, and we both had steady work. We were blessed. Nowadays, the tenants can't afford this land, so they keep on renting. We don't believe people should lose their houses over that. They ought to be able to work something out with Major and his partners."

As though wrapping up their presentation, Mrs. Taylor stood up and smiled. "I think I hear Kevin now. We'll have some supper, but I just want to say we hope the paper will support our position on the development. I know the McCullers are partners in it, but that doesn't make it right."

Another new piece of information. The Big Boys were investors in this. I wondered if they also were involved in Mossy Bend.

Marcus Taylor stood up, too. "God has given us this beauty, and we must be good stewards of it. And we must take care of the poor. That's what the Bible says."

Just then the front door opened and a striking young woman walked in wearing a white lab coat and carrying a pretty leather purse. "Oh, Daddy," the woman said, laughing and walking over to hug Mr. Taylor. "Are you preaching again?"

Her father returned the hug warmly, and her mother stepped up for an embrace of her own. For a moment they were a tight circle, and I was moved by their affection for one another, moved and isolated.

"You must be Lois," the woman said. "I'm Kevin Taylor, lucky enough to be the daughter of this pair." She winked. "And a de facto member of the Lakeside Neighborhood Association. I don't contribute much to their group, but I sure get some good suppers out of the deal. I would shake your hand but I need to wash my hands before I pass on any more germs."

Kevin Taylor? *Kevin* Taylor? Where had I heard

that name? My mind went into its computer search mode, hoping the "find" function came up with something quickly. She wore a lab coat. She carried an expensive handbag. She was affiliated with the Lakeside group.

Aha! Alex had mentioned her, something about her wanting to build a house and getting turned down. Now I remembered.

"Our baby girl made a doctor and came home to Green to look after us," her father said proudly. "We told her she should stay down in Houston or move to Atlanta or Dallas where there are more opportunities, but she insisted on coming home."

It was clear that having his daughter home made his world immensely better, and I wished I had spent more time with my mother before she died—and that I could better remember my own father. Kidney failure killed him when I was only seven.

When Kevin surfaced, she smelled of Dove soap, had combed her hair, and shed the jacket. She was an extremely attractive woman in her late twenties or early thirties and one of the warmest people I had ever met, a woman who seemed comfortable in her own skin.

Our supper will stand forever on my list of memorable meals. We had roast beef and gravy, cooked all day in a Crock-Pot, rice, some peas Mrs. Taylor had put up last summer, and a tomato mix called "chowchow." She had made that, too, and the bread-and-butter pickles and the biscuits.

It had been weeks since I had a home-cooked meal, and I hoped I was not making pig noises.

We opened with a lengthy blessing by Mr. Taylor, praying for everyone from the world's leaders in their quest for peace to schoolteachers and students and brotherly love. He made special mention of Kevin and her healing ministry and his two other girls and their families and then prayed that I might have wisdom as I sojourned in Green. It was a very moving prayer, although I did seriously consider sneaking a bite of biscuit to tide me over.

As we ate, Mrs. Taylor told me to call her Pearl and to call her husband Marcus. They somehow seemed a bit too distinguished for that, and so I began to call them Miss Pearl and Mr. Marcus, just like that.

Much of our conversation revolved around Kevin and me. I was curious about her name and her profession. She wanted to know about my background and how I was doing in Green. She asked the second question as though she knew the answer could go in either direction. She seemed to be asking how things were going beneath the surface, where the real action in Green happened.

Miss Pearl told the story of naming Kevin. "Her daddy already had two daughters and thought this baby was going to be his boy. He chose the name of his younger brother who had been killed in the

Korean War. When Baby Girl Number Three arrived, he was not to be swayed." At this point, Mr. Marcus jumped in. "Besides, I figured this surprise gal was going to do something special with her life and having a man's name couldn't hurt a bit."

Kevin laughed during much of the story, saying it had certainly made life interesting. "I am on some pretty wild mailing lists," she said, "ranging from Viagra advertisements to *Playboy* subscription offers. You just wouldn't believe what can happen when people think you're a man."

"So you have a private practice here?" I asked.

"I'm in a two-person family practice office with a physician who wants to retire in a year or two. He needed a partner badly, and not that many young docs want to move to towns like Green. I've been back for almost two years. You should see what happens when new patients walk in." But she told the story without a trace of bitterness, as though she understood she was a different kind of doctor for this little town.

Part of what made that meal so good was the food, part was the talk, sitting around a table in a real home, visiting, laughing. The business of the association had been temporarily set aside, and I was there as a newcomer to town, someone who needed a warm welcome during this cool season. I did not want to leave. This was the first place I had felt comfortable in quite a few days.

After supper, we moved back into the living

room for coffee and a frozen pound cake that Miss Pearl had heated, apologizing she didn't have a fresh one for us. As we chatted, the talk turned again to the neighborhood association. I asked Kevin about her house-building experience, and she wrinkled up her face.

"Do we really want to go over that story?" she asked. "It's sort of old news to me."

"If you wouldn't mind . . ." my voice trailed off, and then I started again. "It would help me gain perspective on what's going on. I'm trying to learn as much as I can about the community."

For ten minutes or so, Kevin told about moving back to Green, living with her parents for a few months, and choosing a place to live. "I finally had some money to spend after med school, and I wanted something nice. I guess if I admit it, I wanted people to know I was doing just fine."

The first house she tried to buy was in Mossy Bend, a townhouse right on the water. She went through an open house one Sunday and made an offer on Monday. The owner turned her down flat. So on Tuesday she met his price, determined to have that house.

"The next day he took it off the market," she said, twisting her face up again. "Said his sister and brother-in-law were moving back to town in a few months and were going to live there."

"The house sat vacant for several months and then went back on the market and sold to a young white couple. It was pretty clear Mossy Bend wasn't ready for people like us," Marcus Taylor said.

"Now, Daddy, we don't know that," Kevin said, but she reached out and patted his leg.

"Then I decided to build a house, over near the motel, on some property Mama and Daddy own. I hired an architect and adapted plans for one of those great houses that sit up on stilts. But the zoning commission wouldn't approve my plans. Said it was too close to the lake, and drainage wasn't adequate. I redid the plans and pushed the house site back. They turned me down again. Now six months later they plan to build a whole slew of houses like that, in almost the same place."

She smiled, but her words had taken on a little bite. "Now I rent a house across the street in the black part of town," she said, emphasizing the last words. "It only has one bathroom and no central heat or air, but the neighbors don't mind having me. And I sure am saving a lot of money."

"But that's wrong," I said. "That's blatant discrimination. How can they get away with that?"

"Things have been done a certain way in Green for many years," her father said.

"I know something will open up," Kevin said, shrugging. "These things have a way of working out when the time is right."

Suddenly the Taylor house didn't seem so cozy. I needed to get back to the newspaper and work on the mayor's retirement story with Alex.

10

*Red carcasses fill pails next to the picnic
benches at the home of Mayor Oscar Myers.
"This is what I live for," the ninety-two-
year-old mayor said, ripping the head off a
crawfish. "Mudbug season is here, and every
year we invite the entire neighborhood. This
year it's bigger and better than ever."*

—The Green News-Item

While my early days in Green seemed to crawl
by, the next couple of months flew. It was as
though someone had taken my life off slow
motion and put it on fast forward. My mind was
jammed so full of new information that I didn't
know what to do. I practically lived at the newspaper office.

People came out of the woodwork to talk to me
about this problem or that. They included Miss
Barbara Beavers, dress shop owner and regular
advertiser: "I do not like the way my ads look.
They are smeared, and you can't tell the difference between the house coats and the evening
gowns."

And Bud Dillon, "no relation to Matt, ma'am,"
who wrote a folksy farming column. "We need
more agriculture coverage. It's the backbone of

our country. People depend on *The News-Item* for farm prices and new varieties of soy beans and such."

Some people, like Bud, were friendly characters who made living in Green richer and worthwhile. Others, like Miss Barbara, could be mean-spirited and bossy.

In addition, I was soon called upon by a number of special-interest groups, the number and variety a surprise to me in such a small place. "Can you help us with our literacy fund-raiser?" "Can we count on your support for the Catfish Festival?" "Would you make a donation to the Friends of the Confederacy?"

Many meetings began with polite civility and deteriorated into my feeling evil and misunderstood. "We don't think we are getting the coverage we might expect," one club would say. "The newspaper's position is clearly biased," another would complain.

From our position on zoning to litter control, we drew criticism. What distressed me was how many people seemed to think you were a bad person if you disagreed with them. "We can disagree without being disagreeable" became one of my least favorite phrases, since it generally preceded the newspaper getting blasted with both barrels.

Mercifully, these meetings were punctuated by the "social callers," those who wanted to say hello and welcome me to town. They often brought a cake or produce or flowers from their yards. "We want you to know how happy we are to have you in Green." "We'd love to have you speak to our garden club." "This is the recipe that won first place at our Homemaker's Tea. We hope you enjoy it and our community."

At first I tried to refuse the small gifts, citing the age-old newspaper conflict of interest issue. However, Iris Jo and Tammy intervened, telling me that refusing was seen as arrogant or "uppity"—Tammy's word.

"Just go ahead and accept them graciously and share them," Tammy said. "I hardly think Gertrude Lindsey is trying to buy you with that batch of brownies."

Some of these individuals became friends, mentors of sorts. They dropped by, or I would run into them on the street, heading into the library or at the grocery store. They would occasionally send me a handwritten note with a word of praise.

Lots of them invited me to church, but I put them off. "I'm still settling in," I said.

In between all the community meetings, I decided to meet with every person on my payroll and see what we might do to make the newspaper better and maybe make the Green area a better place to live. I considered this Step Two in unloading the paper in a few months, following

Step One of relocating to Green and Step Three of moving away from Green.

My first such meeting was with the news staff—all two of them, plus Tammy, who seemed to have a hand in every department. The part-time photographer didn't show up. "He works for advertising," Alex said.

We sat down with sandwiches and soft drinks, and Tom immediately spoke. "I'd like to write editorials," he said, chewing noisily. "For every edition, the way we used to. I can sign up community columnists, too, to give their side of the story."

Up until shortly before Ed bought the paper, *The News-Item* had used old-fashioned country correspondents, and we decided to bring those back, mostly older women who wrote about comings and goings in their tiny communities.

We roped Tammy into lining those up. She worked the phones like a telemarketer from a major corporation and collected a long list of citizens who produced local news for ten bucks a column. "Dr. and Mrs. Ricky Coffey welcomed out-of-town guest from Waco, Texas, over Easter weekend." "Estelle Gardner celebrated her ninetieth birthday with five generations at her table." "The Daisy Fellowship Garden Club invites you to its gumbo supper. All proceeds will go to maintain wildflower areas in the city." They even helped us cover the all-important local sports, from city leagues to high school games.

Alex was not to be left out during the planning discussion. "I want to do more investigative projects. I'm telling you, something's up with zoning. I can't quite pin it down, but I'm getting tips about Major Wilson and the McCullers and the projects they're handling. Plus, I'm hearing a lot of buzz about the proposed route for the new interstate highway."

Tammy interrupted. "I hear we're getting a Red Lobster."

"That's not true," Tom said. "Green doesn't have liquor by the drink, and they said they won't come without a change in our liquor laws."

"That's not what I hear," Tammy said, with a sniff. And so our first planning meeting went.

One of my rising expenses was paying for public records, a luxury I had taken for granted in my former life. Sometimes I would see Alex's car in the parking lot at the paper late into the evening or find him sifting through official papers when I came in after a community function.

These community functions were mostly new to me. While I had gotten out some in Dayton, my primary role had been in the newsroom. The workflow and news cycle had often interfered with my attending events—and I had been proud of keeping an arm's length between newsmakers and me. Here it was different.

My phone rang steadily. "We'd like to invite you to our annual banquet, Miss Lois," a club or business would say. "We'll have a place for you at the head table." The calls also came when I could not make it. "Dub and Chuck always found time to attend," a civic club president said. "Our members will be so disappointed that you won't be there."

In between all of this, I was doing some digging of my own, still trying to get to the real story on the newspaper's finances. I had learned in journalism school to follow the money to the heart of a story, and used this approach at work. I relentlessly analyzed spreadsheets and went to Iris Jo with questions.

Mostly Lee Roy, my money man, stayed out of my way, unless I trapped him in his office. Sometimes I thought he deliberately went the other way when he saw me coming.

"Oh, Lois, just heading out to make sales calls," he often said. "Need to go check some racks" was another of his lines. I finally forced him to sit down with me and go over a list of advertisers and tried to chart a budget for the third and fourth quarters of the year, an exercise that seemed to displease Lee Roy on every level.

"We've been doing it the other way for years," he said, with a sneer. "It works. Why go fooling around with it when it works?"

"Lee Roy, I have to know more about what is coming in." I felt my face getting warm. "The last time I looked, my name was on the bank loan."

For some reason during this conversation, Pastor

Jean's sermon that first week in Green popped into my mind. She had said God gives us wisdom to do what we're supposed to do. After Lee Roy stalked out, I dug around in a stack of papers on my desk and found the notes I jotted that day. "God guides you, no matter who you are. He surrounds you with love and mercy. He provides answers when the questions are hard." I sure hoped so.

One of the questions I had on my mind was about the girl Katy, and I finally remembered to ask Iris Jo about her. Iris looked solemn and then slowly started talking, her voice quivering slightly.

"Katy's somewhat troubled." She paused. "She's mad at her mother for remarrying after the death of her father a couple of years ago. Then she lost her boyfriend, Matt, in a bad car wreck out near the church."

Iris Jo rummaged around on the top of her desk and pulled out the obituary, which was dated less than a year ago.

"He was a good boy," she said, tears filling her eyes. "They said he was driving too fast, swerved, overcorrected, and hit a tree coming home from Katy's house. He went to church, was one of those boys you think is going to amount to something. Katy quit coming to church for quite a while after that, and I notice her hanging around downtown smoking. That's a hard thing for a girl her age . . . and so soon after her Daddy."

Iris Jo looked up at me as though sizing me up somehow.

"He was my son."

Stunned, I did not know what to say, but I felt tears in my eyes and dabbed at them. I leaned over and hugged her. "Oh, Iris Jo, I am so, so sorry."

"I don't know why the Lord took him," she said, the tears falling more steadily now, "but I know he's in a better place, and one of these days I'll see him again."

Frozen, I stood by her desk.

"You remember when you asked me one time why I wasn't more bothered about the sale of the family paper?" she asked. "What I didn't say is that I've learned that most of the stuff that bothers us just isn't worth the energy."

Right then the phone rang, and I had never been as happy to be interrupted in my life.

As I went into my office, I thought back over how Iris Jo was cheerful, but in a gentle, kind way. She was not an exuberant woman, and I saw now she was still trying to thaw from her unspeakable grief. How could I be near someone for hours on end and not realize how much hurt she held inside? I thought of Katy, too, and wondered if she hung around the paper because Iris Jo was there.

Going to Route 2 that night, my heart felt heavy. I cried when I drove by Iris's house.

Settling into the house in the country was tougher than I expected, harder than settling into the newspaper. I slowly unpacked my belongings and tried unsuccessfully to make it feel like home. Nearly two full weeks passed before I spent a night there, always coming up with excuses to stay at the Lakeside.

"I don't have my phone yet," I said to Iris Jo, "and you know how lousy the cell service is." "Oh, I just like visiting with your mother at the motel," I told Kevin. "It's convenient, and everything at home is such a mess," I said to Tammy.

During my first week of staying at the house, members of the church began showing up—almost like they had been on a stakeout, waiting to see my car overnight in the driveway. The casserole brigade brought supper two or three nights that week, delicious homemade food delivered in Pyrex dishes with names written on masking tape on the bottom. An older man came over, volunteering to help break down the boxes piled on the screened front porch. Someone had cleaned up my yard, and Iris Jo told me it was Chris Craig.

"That name doesn't ring a bell," I said, puzzled over who would do something so nice.

"He's that good-looking catfish farmer down the road, a coach at the school," she said. "He's a regular volunteer at Grace Community. His wife died of breast cancer three years ago. He took up catfish farming as a hobby of sorts—really super person."

"Oh . . . I remember meeting him. The guy you were hugging at church. Do you two date?" I clearly knew little about Iris Jo's personal life.

"Good heavens, no!" she said, almost snorting. "He's more like a son or a brother to me. I wish he could find a good woman."

Touched by everyone's help, I didn't let on that I was afraid to stay way out in the country by myself. It was so alien from my city life, which I found myself yearning for on a regular basis. I longed for my condo. I missed the crazy busy newsroom and my comfort zone. I began to think of relocating when my year was up, to New York or Chicago, a big city with lots going on and fewer people nosing into my business.

Other than spending nights there, in the first few months I spent as little time as possible at the house, almost moving into my office, with a supply of microwavable food and some of my favorite pieces of art.

"Good grief, Miss Lois," Tammy said. "How are Iris Jo and I supposed to look good with the new boss if we always get here after you do and leave before you?" She even devised a contest to see who could get me out of the building earlier, but after a few weeks gave up.

Long evening phone calls with Marti became my habit, helping me put off going home. One Friday night she finally challenged me on it.

"I've got a date with that new guy in marketing

and have got to get off this phone," she said. "You have to get a life."

I pretended to be indignant, but I knew what she meant. That night I rolled up my sleeves and began to transform the country house into my home. I emptied boxes and placed books neatly on shelves, with the hope the Grace cardboard ministry guy would come back by to help me. I hung pictures and pulled out knick-knacks and lined up my antique pottery collection.

The next morning I cleaned and polished, appreciating how the light gave everything a kind of soft glow.

Coffee cup in hand, I walked around the yard and noticed how a few things were already beginning to bud. My mother and grandmother had taught me a lot about flowers, some of it by osmosis. A flowering quince was in bloom, as was a large, healthy forsythia. Several patches of what we called daffodils but local people were calling jonquils were in bloom.

My neighbor and his three mutts drove by in his beat-up pickup truck. He gave a short beep of the horn and waved.

For a moment, I felt settled.

11

"Please keep my aunt Johnnie Pruitt in your
prayers as she recovers from a four-wheeler
accident last weekend. Although I won't
publicize how old she is, Aunt Johnnie admits
she was born the year Huey Long was first
elected governor. She has never had a driver's
license and said it was high time she learned.
'I wanted to take my son's toy for a spin,'
she said. 'I'm tired of sitting out here
in the country by myself.' "

—*The Green News-Item*

I am not sure what surprised me more about
spring in North Louisiana—that it was so incredibly beautiful or that it passed so quickly. Over a
period of just a couple of weeks, everything
exploded in beauty and color, from dogwood
trees that dotted the woods on my way to work to
huge, heirloom azaleas that made old streets
downtown look like tourist attractions.

For weeks now I had described Green to out of
town friends and relatives as shabby without the
chic. Suddenly the town looked groomed,
planned—special. Even the forlorn Lakeside
Annex neighborhood looked better, with big old
bushes bursting out in bloom.

After my years of one plant on the patio, I discovered something new in my yard every time I turned around. The sturdy little tree in the front yard was a pink dogwood. The woods on the edge of my back yard were dotted with pinkish purplish trees called redbuds. It was like living in some sort of home and garden show.

As quickly as it came, it went.

Two days after we ran a photo layout of beautiful yards, complete with our first reader-submitted photos, we got a heavy rain and most of the blooms were knocked off the azaleas. The yellow pollen that had covered everything was washed away.

"That I do not miss," I told Marti. "It freaked me out at first—my nose started itching, my eyes watering, and suddenly everything around town was covered with yellow dust. The car wash on the edge of town even gave pollen checks, instead of rain checks. Can you believe that?"

"Sounds like local color to me," she said with a laugh. "Not your average boring town."

"There could certainly be worse places to spend a year," I said. "There's something about my house where I can relax and be myself. I've met so many nice people in the past few months, too. None of them are you, of course, but they're good people."

The spring weather had a softening effect on lots of people, as though they were coming out of hibernation. The winter had not been bad at all, certainly not by Midwest standards, but the days had often been gray and chilly. Downtown, always a bit frayed around the edges, perked up with springtime.

More people were "stirring around," as local residents liked to say. The library, where I had become a regular customer, was busier, ranging from older people learning to use the Internet to school kids working on term papers. The drug store put up a fascinating spring display of photographs of graduating seniors.

The Holey Moley Antique Mall even gained several new vendors. Over my first few months in Green, the owners, Rose Parker and Linda Murphy, the Linder who worked for Major, became two of my closest acquaintances. They pieced the business together around their busy lives and seemed pleased when they made a ten-dollar sale. I wondered sometimes how they paid the rent.

"God always provides," Rose said on a regular basis. She was one of those people who believe things will turn out right, offsetting Linda's perpetual glumness. "I know the good Lord is looking out for us today. It's amazing how things come together."

Rose had grown up in Green, was married to a farmer twenty years her senior, and was the hardest-working woman I had ever met. She was also the mail carrier out on Route 2. "I know who you're getting love letters from and who you owe," she said, with a smile.

"No love letters," I said. "Only bills."

Linda had joined the Holey Moley partnership with caution. She was a woman who did not expect things to turn out well, probably with good reason. She was miserable working at Major's office but needed the benefits. How she stuck with the job, I could not figure out, slowly learning how badly he behaved, barking orders, snapping at her and treating her like dirt.

"He's just mean as a snake," Rose said. "Mean as a snake."

Linda had been single for years, after marrying a "sloppy drunk" when she was just out of high school. The men she dated were invariably losers who hurt her in some way. Her latest boyfriend had broken a date with her on a Saturday, right after I first met her, and remarried his ex-wife the next Wednesday.

"I'm not white trash," she told me once, "but I act like white trash."

Linda's parents were in terrible physical health, and her mother had dementia. "Half the time she doesn't know me any more," Linda said. "And she's doing things like putting her bra on over her church dress and calling to ask if I've seen Boots. That cat died twenty years ago."

Once more I realized the terrible burdens most people carry around every day.

Rose and Linda admitted during one of our first conversations that they knew little about marketing. They used a couple of my ideas to build the Holey Moley's business, but struggled to get people from the interstate to downtown.

Sitting in my office one day, I stared out at a line of snowy white Bradford pear trees along the edge of the newspaper's property, and it hit me. Why couldn't *The News-Item* lead an effort to bring back downtown, to get people to clean up their property and to shop in their hometown? What would it take to make downtown vibrant again? Maybe this was a way I could make a difference in this little community.

The pretty spring and the short burst of increased interest in the area had given me a glimpse of something new in Green, an indefinable characteristic that almost felt like hope. Even though *The News-Item* only had a dozen employees, we were one of the biggest businesses downtown, plus we had a small measure of clout in town, mostly from the social standing of the McCullers.

"We can use the power of the newspaper to try to rally residents," I said to Tom. He seemed delighted, ready to tackle an editorial crusade.

"We can tie that into profiles of downtown businesses," Alex said. "We can also examine how the area got into such rotten shape and how it might get out." He paused. "Maybe you could even splurge and let me visit a similar place or two that have turned their downtowns around."

Visiting with Rose one Saturday, I broached the idea of forming a Downtown Green Association. She was initially excited about the possibility but deflated fairly quickly after talking to Linda.

"We tried something like that once, and it didn't work," Linda said. This was another of those sentences I'd learned to despise. The number of things Green had tried before with bad results confounded me. To hear local people talk, nothing had gone right since about 1959.

I took a deep breath and persisted. "What could it hurt to try again? We could just get together with some snacks and visit about new ideas. I'm new. You have new vendors. Maybe we could even talk Eva Hillburn into coming."

My contact with Eva had been minimal, but I had learned she was quite important in Green. Very little happened without her stamp of approval. She was deeply involved behind the scenes in local politics and a generous donor to many nonprofits. Although her older brother had the public persona, I'd come to believe Eva was probably more powerful.

Setting up the first meeting took some doing, but I managed to pull it off. We gathered in the boardroom of the newspaper and had box lunches from the Cotton Boll. I almost felt like I was back in Dayton, except the boxes had smiley faces drawn on them with a black marker and a note with each person's order.

Eva arrived late, but she did show up. Rose was out delivering the mail, but Linda was there, along with Iris Jo and a variety of others from downtown businesses. Pastors from the big Baptist and Methodist churches downtown came, including Pastor Mali, the new foreign guy wearing his native dress, a *tepenu*. His arrival in town had caused somewhat of a stir, and I always enjoyed seeing his cheerful face. Lee Roy did not bother to show up, a point I planned to challenge.

"Let's open with a quick recap of what has been done before and how we can build on that," I said, after thanking everyone for coming.

"I beg your pardon, Miss Lois," one of the bankers said. "We haven't had our prayer yet."

This was something that intrigued me about Green. People had not gotten ashamed of their religion down here. The prayer, by the Baptist preacher, was almost poetic, including asking God to "look after Miss Lois and help her as she tries to guide us." I was always overwhelmed at how quick people were to pray for me, and I thought the words set just the tone we needed for the meeting. In fact, I got so wrapped up in the idea that I asked Pastor Mali from the Methodist church to close us in prayer.

From that meeting, we made progress with fits and starts. At first members got hung up on a name and mission statement, but Eva moved us along. "Friends," she said with a firm but friendly tone to her voice, "we need to make something happen. Downtown Green needs our action."

In just a handful of meetings, we came up with what we called our Green Forward Goals, which quickly became the GFGs. These included a downtown cleanup day, a special Fourth of July ice cream social and sale day, and a Fall Festival the first weekend of October.

Sometimes I would notice Eva watching me with a serious look on her face, but she seldom had much to say to me. She was out of town a lot and extremely busy, so I was always happy to see her arrive. Something about her presence gave the group some heft.

After the third meeting, she stopped on her way out. "Lois, I'd like to invite you to dinner with me at the country club one night. I apologize for not connecting with you sooner, welcoming you properly to town."

I hesitated before I said "yes." I had been to the Oak Crest Country Club several times already, always on business, usually courting an advertiser with Lee Roy. I did not find it very welcoming. In part, the décor looked like something out of the mid-1950s, with heavy drapes, sea foam green walls, white linen tablecloths, and a parquet dance floor. Beyond that, it seemed snooty. I owned a business and was approaching middle age, but I felt like a kid eating at the grown-up table.

However, I could not turn Eva down after all she had done for Green Forward and the newspaper. "Sure, I'd love to go," I said, smiling. "That'll be great."

Wearing a nice outfit I bought from Miss Barbara, who was still complaining about her ads, I met Eva on Saturday night. We were seated at a table in the corner, far enough away from the combo playing sixties songs. We each ordered sweet iced tea. I noticed with a small measure of amusement that several vocal people in the local anti-liquor-by-the-drink campaign were having wine, beer, or a strawberry daiquiri with their meals. Maybe the newspaper should do a story on where liquor was sold and consumed in the parish.

As we ate, Eva told me again how glad she was to have me in Green.

"I enjoy watching you lead the downtown group," she said. "I can't believe it, but I'm thinking we may get something done this go-round. You are something when you go into action." She hesitated. "I hope I don't sound patronizing when I say that you have the gift of leadership. You are a bright spot in our community."

I almost choked on my tea and covered the sound with a little cough that came out more like a hiccup. One of the things I most enjoyed about my new job was it brought me in touch with such a wide range of people. Earlier that day I been trying to convince Rose to put a billboard on the interstate and to add a regional crafts booth to her store. Tonight I was dining with the most influential businesswoman in town, and she was paying me a gigantic compliment.

"Thank you," I said, "but I think you are the one with that gift. I admire you and what you do for the Green area."

Immediately she blew that off in her elegant, somewhat old-fashioned way of speaking. "I'm obligated to give back to Green because it has given so much to me and my family through the years," she said. "I've had to work for lots in my life, but I've had many opportunities other people never have. I don't take that for granted."

Dabbing a tiny blob of Thousand Island dressing from the corner of her mouth, she continued. "As I was saying, I believe deeply that to whom much is given, much is expected. That is part of why I asked you here tonight. I want to know if you'd consider helping me stir things up."

12

Betty Brosette's dog, Elfie Smith, remains missing and has been at-large since Thursday. He had not been found at press time. Betty lives off Old Bayou Boulevard, and so did Elfie Smith, a mixed breed that most of you know: white, brown ears and feet, loves liver and tomatoes, which you remember from a story we published and ran in May.

—The Green News-Item

"*News-Item*, Lois Barker," I said, picking up my phone on a day when it had not stopped ringing.

The McCullers had called to complain about a package we had done on proposed roadwork near the lake. Major Wilson contended we were ruining his business with our negative coverage, and Lee Roy had rushed into my office, demanding to know if I meant to completely kill our revenue streams.

"You are some firecracker, aren't you?" a gruff, sort of wavery woman's voice said on the phone, a voice that sounded old but not the least bit unsure.

"I beg your pardon?"

"Miss Barker, you are stepping on toes right and

left in this town, and I can't tell you how much fun it is to watch."

"May I help you, ma'am?" I said, surprised at how close to the surface my old irritated city editor voice was.

"Oh, get off your high horse, missy. This is Helen McCuller, and I wanted to thank you for dusting off my history of the community and running that piece. It reminded me of the days when I was the one stirring things up."

"Oh, Aunt Helen!" I said, then immediately realized what I had done. "I mean Miss McCuller, how good it is to hear from you. I apologize for not contacting you before the history ran. I've been meaning to call. The feedback has been outstanding."

"Well, girl, I'm glad it worked out, and you just call me Aunt Helen. Most people in town do."

"I want to thank you for all you did at your house, too," I said. "You probably know I'm living out on Route 2 now. That yard is something else."

"Did the dogwood bloom? Last time I was out that way it looked like the cold had nipped it back a little."

Helen's call lasted nearly an hour. Before it was over, I had a new supporter, which meant a lot in a month when I was turning people off right and left. "Don't worry about big people with little minds," she said. "And don't take the politics of life in Green too seriously. Local politics are seldom as good as they could be, nor as bad as they seem."

She suggested I drop by to see her sometime. "Keep fighting, firecracker."

While I had never thought of myself as a firecracker, my role in Green did suddenly seem to be that of troublemaker, ranging from annoying half the businesses in town with the Downtown Dollar Days to attempting to become the first female member of the Oak Crest Country Club.

Eva, who had led me into part of this stink, told me it had always bothered her that the country club, such an integral part of Green life for movers and shakers, had never invited women as members. "I'm an ex-officio member, through my family connections, but I am not a voting member," she said. "I find that insulting. And I am quite troubled that there are not members of color."

This topic clearly mattered to her. "How can we as community members—as Christian people—shut out one of the biggest groups in our community? And if you try to tell me that they like to hang out with people of their own kind, I'll throw up my tilapia right here."

I had not known for certain that the club excluded minorities and women but had suspected it. For the past six months or so, I had been funding Lee Roy's membership, knowing in my heart it was wrong. "This is immoral and unethical," Eva said, "and I need your help in getting Dr. Kevin Taylor to seek membership, too. She's the perfect person to be our first minority member."

I sighed, half out of frustration that we were still living divided by skin color, and half because I did not need nor want another battle. For the first time in several weeks I thought of Ed and wondered how the sixty-year-old, white male would have handled this. But I knew I couldn't squirm out of it, no matter how uncomfortable it made me.

Eva was a bit too gleeful when I said I would be her female guinea pig.

Kevin came along more slowly.

"I'm just not sure," she said. "I don't want to stir things up . . . but I would like to see our town be more accepting."

I jumped in. "If we don't take a stand, who will? This is really a small thing, and it could help in big ways later on."

"I wouldn't even consider it if that house issue hadn't come up," she said. "I just can't believe you can't buy a house somewhere because you're black." She finally agreed to apply for membership. The three of us had lunch at the club to seal the deal, a meal that got more attention than it should have.

I also implemented an aggressive community outreach program to get lots of different people in the paper, making it more representative of the

141

parish as a whole. I had to do this because it was the job of the newspaper to reflect the area, and I had to do it from a business standpoint.

"We need to be more open about asking for news and opinions from different groups," I told each of the small staff. "And we need to be helpful in publishing it in a timely and fair way." The coverage prompted a wave of calls that we were running too many blacks in the paper and I would be the ruin of the town. Only two or three of my older "coaches" called to tell me I was doing the right thing, ranging from Miss Gertrude with another pound cake to Miss Pearl.

The former owners and my business manager were not as kind, chiming in for the second time in less than a week. The Big Boys stopped by together, something unprecedented since the day I took over *The News-Item*. They seemed determined to make me change my mind about the country club and the kinds of news we put in the paper, subtly reminding me I was a short-timer in Green and should not make a fuss.

"Miss Lois, we're sure you mean well," Dub said, "but you are sticking your nose in something that doesn't really concern you. This has long-term implications for our little town. Things are working fine just like they are."

Chuck jumped in as soon as Dub paused. "This is the South, and things just aren't done like they are up north . . . bad for business."

When they left, they were annoyed I had not readily agreed with them.

"I'm trying to do what's best," I said. "What's right. I'll keep considering the best steps to take—for the paper and for Green."

Lee Roy's eyes nearly popped out of his head when I told him what I was doing, in the community and the newspaper. I also told him if Kevin and I did not get into Oak Crest, I would cancel his membership, unwilling to contribute to a business that was unfair.

Not thirty minutes passed before I had another call from Major.

"Miss Lois, I'm calling as your friend to tell you to let things stay the way they are. People pay for their memberships, and they have the right to invite whoever they want to join. If someone does not want to join because of club policies, that's his or her choice."

I waited for him to continue, certain the pause was not the end of his speech.

"Those people have all sorts of clubs that let them in," he said.

My voice trembled when I answered him, but I hoped it did not show. I acted as though I had totally misunderstood his point.

"I look forward to your support on this issue," I said, "knowing you represent so many of the fine people of Green in your police jury district, women and men, African Americans and Whites.

I know that as a Realtor and a public official you do not believe in discrimination because of the color of someone's skin or their gender. I'd appreciate you reminding your friends at Oak Crest of that."

And I hung up on him.

It was the only time in Green I ever hung up on anyone. I was not proud of myself, but I did not want him to know I was crying. His call came just after I had taken a contentious call from a preacher who told me how wrong I was. The two combined were too much. Between offending people by trying to bring some equality to Green and offending small-town businesses by "playing favorites," I was homesick for the anonymity of the city desk at a big paper.

Several downtown businesses had gotten their feelings hurt that they were not included in a group advertisement we ran, promoting the upcoming Homemade Ice Cream Social and Downtown Dollar Days. The other bank, where the paper did not have its accounts, complained to the chamber of commerce that I was trying to "take over," and the chamber should do something about it. While some people, such as the Baptists and Methodists, seemed thrilled and were planning downtown activities for children every Saturday in July, others were annoyed and thought the efforts a waste of time and energy. The grumblers came out in full force.

I was discouraged, but not deterred.

I had expected this to be a tough job and a rough year, but I was stunned by how raw some of the issues left me, how I doubted myself and the people around me. Over and over I asked myself if I was doing the right thing, if it was my right to try to change this little town where I was basically a visitor. I cried to my dead mother and asked what she would do. I sought out like-minded people to tell me I was doing the right thing, and people who disagreed with me to try to talk sense into me. I thought about Pastor Jean's sermon on wisdom and tried to figure out what she might have been telling me.

In the end, I prayed—deep, heartfelt, on-my-knees prayer, for the first time since the day my mother was buried.

Amazingly, interesting dominoes began to fall. First Methodist Church pastors had traditionally been members of Oak Crest, but now the pastor was a foreign man who never wore a suit and sometimes still wore what looked like a skirt. He did, however, like to play golf. His church leaders stepped forward to recommend him for the church's membership slot at the club and included a letter announcing their support of the membership of Miss Lois Barker and Dr. Kevin Taylor. The congregation at Grace Community Chapel, most of whom had only been to a wedding reception or high school reunion at the club, wrote a moving letter, signed by nearly thirty-five members, an accomplishment, considering the average attendance at worship.

Kevin's elderly partner endorsed her with vigor. Although he had expressed some reservations to her in private, in public he told the world such prejudice had to be wiped out. The chamber of commerce wound up endorsing Eva Hillburn as a full member, pointing out her leadership stature.

By the time we were voted in, the country club battle seemed somewhat shallow and the victory a bit hollow. But Aunt Helen stopped by the newspaper to meet me face-to-face and remind me history was being made.

"It takes brave people to stand against a crowd," she said, holding out her wrinkled hand to shake mine. "I'm proud of you, girl. When you taking me out there for lunch?"

I had little time to go to the club now that I was a member because of the upcoming festivities downtown. I worked with Tom on our Green Forward editorials and invited each of the downtown merchants to write a short guest column about why they liked being part of the heart of Green. I hired a freelance artist to design a cute map of downtown that could run in the paper and be distributed by each business. Tammy went on a building-wide cleaning campaign that was astounding in its results, and Iris Jo organized newspaper tours for the day of the Ice Cream Social.

The event had turned into a fund-raiser to buy sidewalk benches and to replace a few hideous modern streetlights with expensive old-fashioned ones that suited the character of the town better. The occasion had begun to pick up steam, literally, since the July weather was the hottest on record.

Kevin called. "I can do free blood-pressure checks in the lobby of the paper," she said. Someone from the school board office called. "May we have a table for school registration dates, the Parent-Student Association and other education news?" The high school athletic booster club had leftover spirit ribbons they wanted to sell. The Green Fire Department asked to bring one of its trucks and agreed to shoot fireworks that the chamber had somehow come up with. "We got the art guild to put together a great exhibition," Rose said, "with some very nice work for sale."

The 4-H Club volunteered to do a petting zoo, but we wound up turning down that offer. "Have you ever smelled goats in summer?" a member of Green Forward asked.

"Maybe we'll do something in the fall," I told the nice student who called. I was probably losing my mind even to suggest the fall event, but he seemed so disappointed about not being part of this.

I ran into Katy several times on the streets downtown, and she had begun to be marginally friendlier. She even introduced me to her friend, Molly, an African American girl I had seen getting on and off the school bus near the paper.

"She rescued me from some bullies at school," Katy said, poking the other girl in the ribs. Clearly the two had become good friends before school let out for summer. I wondered sometimes if it were easier for Katy to make a new friend than to try to pretend she wasn't sad around her old friends.

They sat on the loading dock one day, Katy smoking and Molly fiddling with an old CD player. "Hey, girls," I said. "We need some help, and Tammy said you might be the answer. How about running the snow cone stand during our downtown festivities?"

I tried to assess their interest. "You get to keep half of what you make. The other half goes to the downtown fund."

Both girls seemed pleased, as though looking for something to shake off their boredom. During the next few days, they were in and out of the paper a half dozen times, planning with Tammy, asking for materials for signs, copy paper for flyers, tape, and scissors and a variety of other things. Their enthusiasm rubbed off on others at *The News-Item*, and interest in the festivities picked up.

The day of the celebration turned out to be the hottest ever recorded in Green. The newspaper, Eva, and the hardware store had scraped up enough

148

money to buy all the volunteers green T-shirts with "Go Green!" on the front and a list of our downtown association members on the back.

By mid-morning most of the shirts were soaking wet, and volunteers were wiping their faces with the white handkerchiefs still carried by most men in Green.

The homemade ice cream helped. When we tried to count how many dishes of ice cream we served, we would start laughing—"get tickled," as Tammy said—and have to start over. The best I could figure, we had about three dozen ice cream freezers in action, with a backup supply in the freezers at the Cotton Boll Café. Some of the ice cream cooks were purists, turning up their noses at the suggestion they make anything but vanilla. Others were somewhat famous in Green for their Fresh Peach or Butterfinger ice cream. The unofficial taste tests had an underlying competitiveness.

By the middle of the afternoon, the thermometer at the bank read 103. I worried that people might drop from heat exhaustion, but the heat steered more people into businesses. The churches turned on their lawn sprinklers for the children to play in.

The one person who didn't seem hot was Eva, who wore white linen slacks and a sleeveless silk shirt and looked as though she were ready for a day of bridge at the club. The only thing I could find wrong with her was a little lipstick on her front tooth.

"My mother told me that ladies don't sweat," she said with a laugh. "They glow."

"Well, that explains it then," I said. I do not recall ever sweating so much in my life.

Some of the people I had begun to think of as friends made it a point to show up. Pearl and Marcus and most of the members of the Lakeside Neighborhood Association were there, wandering around, meeting and greeting with years of experience. Mr. Marcus ate a Blue Raspberry snow cone, turning his lips and tongue blue and generally distracting from his dignified appearance—one of the funnier things I saw that day.

Aunt Helen arrived in a nursing home van with a half dozen other women and stayed for an hour before it got too hot. "You did it," she said. "You drew a crowd downtown. Fine work."

Several of my newspaper regular visitors came and contributed cookies for Tammy to serve in the lobby. Even the usual local politicians showed up, including Mayor Oscar, who had achieved hero status with his retirement announcement, and Major, shaking hands with one arm and wiping his face with the other.

Pastor Jean brought a trio of small boys. "Meet my friends, Miss Lois. They live near the church, and we're having a special day today because they're such special fellows." They looked like urchins from a poor nation, with dirty clothes that were too small and ragged tennis shoes. I bought each of them a snow cone and made sure they got to sit inside the fire truck and sound the siren.

Iris Jo visited nearby with several people at the school tables, including Katy's mother and Craig, the catfish farmer and coach, who smiled and walked over to visit when he saw me. Or was his name Chris?

I was surprised at how happy I was that he had made it.

"Nice to see you again," I said, holding out my hand. "I owe you a big thank-you for cleaning up my yard months ago. I'm sorry I haven't stopped by to say thanks."

His handshake was firm, and his hands calloused. "Good to see you again too. You are one busy lady, aren't you?" He gestured toward all the activities. "Congratulations on pulling this off."

"Oh, lots of people did this. Thanks for coming."

"Iris Jo told me you have been a ball of fire to get this thing going. She said you put it together by sheer force of will. My guys are sure enjoying themselves. They need a little something to do in the summer." He nodded over to where the football team clowned around at the booster table.

"Craig, I mean Chris." I stumbled on his name.

"Two first names," he said. "Happens all the time. No problem."

"Well, anyway, you gave me directions that day out past my house, and you had your dogs with you. I understood Mannix and Kramer, but Markey?"

"Markey Post, the actress. My brother loved her and named my puppy for her."

Just then Katy came up to ask where to find more ice. "Hey, coach," she said. "Want to buy a snow cone?"

The two of them walked off, and I shook my head, amazed at how connected I suddenly felt to so many people.

As I stood there, Rose came up and gave me a big hug. "We're having our best day ever at the Holey Moley," she said. "Thank you so much."

For the rest of the day, I flitted around, thanking people for coming and offering discount subscriptions to the paper. I gave away coupons for free classified ads, passed out surveys asking people to tell us what they wanted to read about, and drew names for door prizes.

If I thought I had been in the middle of things on the city desk in Dayton, I was mistaken. I felt like an air-traffic controller who suddenly gets a chance to take a flight after years in the tower. It was as though I had been sitting on the sidelines before I came to Green, a spectator in my own life.

Being on the field was a lot more intense, harder really, but on most days it was more fun.

13

*Bayou Lake is low due to the recent drought,
but spirits are high because Billy Ray Cyrus
will be here performing his hits from the
early nineties at the Bouef Parish Fair.*

—The Green News-Item

One day I dashed into the post office, and my car wouldn't start five minutes later. "It's the heat," Tammy said, pulling out jumper cables. "It drains the battery faster than anything."

Another day I went out to the parking lot and a long crack had appeared on my windshield, from the bottom almost to the top. "It's the heat," Tom told me. "If you have a little nick in your windshield, it spreads when you have your car shut up on these hot days."

Despite the lack of rain, the heat settled on you like a damp blanket, with humidity soaring. The only laugh I got that week was when Tom said, "You just have to get used to the humisery."

Temperatures topping one hundred and humidity to match consumed conversations—from Bud and his agriculture report to the ladies from the garden club who watered their flowerbeds twice a day.

"You're going to be shocked by the light bill," Stan said one morning.

"I'm wilting on my route," Rose said, moving slowly at the Holey Moley. "My new hobby is tracking how hot it gets in my mail truck."

High school football practice was moved to 5 a.m., and still parents complained. I heard from Iris Jo that Chris had lost lots of his catfish. They died or were too fishy smelling when he took them in to sell.

The lake was so low the beautiful homes at Mossy Bend were sitting up high and dry.

"Having lived through July in Louisiana," I told Marti on the phone, "I thought I could live through anything. I hadn't counted on August."

My yard was cracked and brown, and my flowers barely held on. The hydrangeas that had been so beautiful earlier in the summer wilted and begged for water. When I went out to water, the mosquitoes got after me, apparently the only creatures that flourished in these temperatures. My air conditioner ran nonstop, and I found myself dreading small errands.

Katy proved to be a bright spot during these hot weeks. Since the downtown festival, she had become downright chatty, occasionally popping up in the newspaper parking lot or dropping by my office. Sometimes she would ask me a question about the paper, trying to act as though the answer didn't matter. At other times, she would tell me something going on in Green, something the kids talked about or that she heard at church.

"You coming back to our church?" she asked one day.

"I don't know . . . maybe one of these days when things settle down a little. What brought that up?"

"Pastor Jean asked about you the other day. She saw me and Molly talking to you at the festival, and she asked if we were friends and if I might be able to talk you into visiting the church again. Said we sure could use you."

I made a joke and changed the subject.

People had not let up on trying to get me to church.

"Have you found a church home yet?" was another of those questions I came to dread. Pastors from the big churches downtown kept saying I was "always welcome." Mr. Marcus tried to get me to come speak to his Sunday school class at the Morning Star Baptist Church, and the angry pastor from another town put me on his church newsletter mailing list.

To top it off, Marti was steadily dating a seminary student she had met through a friend of a friend and was church shopping in Dayton. "I am determined to find a place where I fit in spiritually," she said. "I have high hopes for this relationship, and I need to get back to church."

Going to church was a big deal in Green.

"Never plan any kind of community gathering on Wednesday evenings," Tammy said one day at the Holey Moley, "because that's prayer meeting night. You can't stir up a crowd for anything else on a Wednesday."

Linda agreed as she packaged up Tammy's costume jewelry purchase. "If I skip church, I still put on my church clothes to go out to eat. That way people think I attended services."

The staff at the paper planned its vacations around vacation Bible school. It beat anything I had ever seen.

Aunt Helen was what was called locally "a church-going woman," and she often mentioned her faith. Since the festival, we visited every week or so, usually over a meal at the Cotton Boll Café. She asked good questions and listened to my answers, occasionally throwing in a piece of wisdom that immediately put an issue in perspective.

One evening at the diner, I brought up a topic that weighed on me. "I don't understand why so many things are done in shades of gray in Green. How can people live with the double standard, going to church on Sunday but being so mean during the week?"

"Lois, a lot of things in life aren't clear-cut," she said. "People are given choices. That's why God gave us a brain. I think he'd be insulted if we just went along without ever asking questions or trying to figure out a new way of seeing something."

She poured creamer from a tiny plastic container

into her coffee, adamant that caffeine did not keep her awake at night. "Matter of fact, that's one of the things I like about you . . . you're always questioning God."

"I hate to disagree with you, Aunt Helen," I said, "but for once, you are wrong. I don't question God. I ignore him—or her or whatever it is."

Although she was not an overly affectionate woman and one of the few people in Green who did not seem to feel the need to hug, she reached over and touched my hand.

"Sugar, you may not realize it, but you've done nothing but question God since the day you got to town. I would bet good money this started before you got here, maybe right about the time your friend died. I'd say God is working in ways you haven't even begun to imagine."

Our regular waitress stopped at that moment to offer Helen a special bite of cobbler. "We tried this recipe out today," she said, ignoring me. "See what you think."

"Sold!" Helen said, smacking her lips "I'll be back for more."

The waitress usually snapped at me and treated Helen like royalty, going back to our first meal there together.

"She's a Yankee, isn't she?" the woman asked and thrust her order pad in my face. "I might as well tell you right now. We don't do Miracle Whip, and we don't do Pepsi."

Helen helped me make decisions about the paper with her outspoken opinions. I asked her about things I was hesitant to broach with Iris Jo, such as where Lee Roy had come from and his relationship with Major.

"I am not a fan of either of those two," she said when I visited her room one day. "They spend too much time looking after their own interests and never acting on behalf of anyone else. They're thicker than thieves, and you need to keep your eyes open."

"Could you be a bit more specific, please?" I asked. "I mean, do you have any information I can use?"

"I have suspected for years that Lee Roy is stealing from the paper, but I don't have any proof. There's something going on with him that just does not add up. I'm not sure about my nephews. You're a smart thing. You'll figure it out one of these days."

Then she changed the subject. "I wish folks would quit complaining about the blasted weather. It's always hot in August, and I will never understand why people act every year like it surprises them."

During our get-togethers, I also talked about my future.

"I miss the city," I told her one evening. "There was always something going on there. And I miss the big newsroom with all its hustle and bustle. Even the yelling and the cranky copy desk."

She gave one of her trademark harrumphs. "Plenty going on here, too," she said. "But you'll have to be the one to decide where you're supposed to be."

"I admit I've enjoyed this more than I ever thought I would," I said. "I'm even thinking I might want to get on the publisher track somewhere, run one of the big papers. I think I could do it. What do you think?"

"Of course you could do that, but you'll never get rich working for someone else," she said, always adamant about my building financial independence. "You need to take advantage of that keen mind of yours. There isn't some man coming along on a white horse to save you. He'll probably be driving some broke-down pickup and want you to pay the note on a new one."

"Do you think the McCullers should have held onto the paper?"

"Goodness gracious, no," she said, immediately. "Those boys were running that newspaper right into the ground and Green right along with it. You have to have a lot of heart to run a newspaper, a passion of sorts. That's why God sent you down here to us."

"But, Aunt Helen . . ."

She threw up her wrinkled hand. "Shush. No more. You're the right person for this place. It's the right place for you. Now, let's move on."

"Ouch," I said.

"I'm an old woman. I have to speak my mind," she replied.

One evening we saw Katy and her parents leaving the Cotton Boll as we arrived.

"You need to help that girl," Helen said. "Rustle up some work for her. She needs something to keep her out of trouble."

Ashamed that I had not thought of hiring Katy, I ran the idea by Iris Jo, conscious of how the girl's presence might be a reminder of her loss.

"I thought she might write a column for teens, interest them and their parents in the newspaper. It would certainly give her something to focus on and make her a little spending money. Plus, it would be fun to have her around the newsroom," I said in my not-so-subtle sales pitch.

"It would be great to have her here," Iris Jo said. "She needs something to do, and I've always thought she was one of those girls who had special gifts to develop. If there's anything I can do to help, let me know."

When I brought the idea up, however, Katy was immediately cool to it. She had a career path in mind that involved going to beauty school and opening her own shop.

"I am not a brain," she said in that tone of voice she used when I first met her on the loading dock. "You feel sorry for me, don't you? You're just trying to be nice."

As she went on, I could tell she wanted me to talk her into it.

"Katy, I love having you around, so I have to admit that I am trying to be nice. But I also have been watching you for weeks now. You're plugged into everything in town."

I picked up the end of the long, beaded necklace she wore. "You would bring down the stodgy factor of *The News-Item* considerably. You are the ideal combination of local person and fresh voice. We'd pay you, of course. Not much, but enough to help you buy some of that gum to quit smoking."

"I'll think about it," she said and dashed out the door, whether in excitement or anger I could not tell. The next day she was back with a sample column and a notebook with a list of ideas.

"I guess it wouldn't hurt anything if we gave it a try," she said. Her journalism career had begun.

The staff was friendly to her. I worried Alex might be too friendly, his twenty-two years to her sixteen. Katy hung around the newsroom all the time, even when she had already turned in her column or finished a story.

In only a couple of weeks, she decorated her cubicle in her own way, including an old typewriter she bought on a clearance table at the Holey Moley, a thrift shop lamp, and a small picture of Matt. She had an oversized homemade ceramic mug filled with an assortment of pens and pencils in wild colors, and she always had tape and scissors nearby. She was constantly cutting something out of a magazine or one of the city papers and tacking it to her bulletin board.

"That's my idea file," she said.

Tom turned out to be a great writing teacher. He sat patiently with her, showing her when to use active verbs and how to improve transitions in her thoughts.

Eavesdropping the first time or two, I was afraid he would hurt her feelings or that she would snap at him and hurt his. To the contrary, she lit up when he went through her copy, asking questions and making changes with enthusiasm.

One day she stood up, gave him a big hug, and said, "Thank you so much." In my nearly two decades in the newsroom, I don't recall ever seeing a reporter hug an editor for a job well done. Tom and I both nearly fell out. He even started taking a little more care with his appearance, as though maybe he was not at the boring end of his career after all.

When school opened, Katy's devotion to the paper increased. She got the school bus to drop her off right out front most days. I found myself watching for her and worried if she did not show up on schedule.

"You can't believe how hot that bus is," she said nearly every day. "It's unbearable." Her clothes were wet with sweat.

"The A/C doesn't work?" Tom asked.

"A/C?" she shrieked, rolling her eyes. "Like those buses have air-conditioning. What dream world do you live in? The driver told us today it was 119 degrees on our bus. We ought to do an exposé or something on that."

With that pronouncement, she wandered over to the Coke machine, and Tom and I looked at each other. That conversation led to Alex, Tom, Tammy, and I each riding a different bus every afternoon for a week and recording the temperatures, interviewing the driver and students. The results were shocking and made for good news stories and editorials. That coverage led parents to organize a community meeting, demanding the school board come up with a plan to phase in air-conditioned buses over the next three years.

Katy's new column and access to the paper gave her a sort of celebrity status among her classmates, which she fully exploited. "Why don't we start a school society feature?" she asked one day at a staff meeting. "You know, with party pictures and gossip about what kids are doing."

She also told me we needed to add a teen advisory board, similar to the community business group.

"Those downtown people made something happen," she said. "Let's try something with kids. Maybe we can come up with some real news." She walked off, laughing, sounding oddly like bossy Aunt Helen.

I turned Katy loose on the teen project with a "yes" and fifty dollars. Next thing I knew, I was sitting in on meetings of a diverse group of kids whose interests ranged from bow hunting deer to the latest video games. The ideas flew, and Katy was a strict leader, keeping everyone from talking at once. Those ideas turned into features that students wrote and got five bucks each for.

"Could I sell some advertising?" one student asked. "You know, a booster page."

I looked over at Tammy, who often sat in on the meetings. She shrugged.

"Sure," I said. "We'll pay you a commission on whatever you sell."

The decision annoyed Lee Roy when I mentioned it later. "What do you mean? Kids selling advertising? This isn't a game, Lois."

He mumbled under his breath as he left.

Katy added something the paper needed, a young, enthusiastic spark. When she helped Alex look through records, still digging for the elusive fact that would complete the development story, she was excited about any pattern she came up with. When she painted the death names on the front window, she added hearts and flowers and made them look special. When one of her interviews turned out to be especially good, she would burst into the building. "Listen to this, everyone. Listen to what I've got."

On her seventeenth birthday, she got her mother

to bring her by the newspaper before school. "Happy birthday to me," she said, bursting into the newsroom with a box of doughnuts. "In honor of the occasion, free doughnuts with sprinkles!"

And off she went.

Occasionally I would see Iris Jo at Katy's desk or vice versa, the two visiting and sometimes laughing. You could almost feel the healing taking place.

14

Business owner Tommy Carter hopes to hear a peep out of you. Tommy credits the Green Forward program with saving his hardware store and is giving away free chicks as a thank-you. "Old customers are coming back, and we're seeing dozens of new ones," he said. "If y'all come in this week, I'll give you a free gift."

—*The Green News-Item*

An uneasy thought nagged at me.

The year was flying by, and arrangements needed to be made to sell the paper.

At first I put it off, using one excuse or another, ranging from the country club incident to the downtown festival plans to prep football coverage, which I had learned was extremely important to Green readers.

Then my banker, Duke Brazil, brought it up at one of our regular lunch meetings. "What are you thinking, Lois?" he asked. "How can the bank help you with this?'

I had put it off as long as I could.

The paper was making a decent profit, although we were not blowing the roof off. Still, it would probably be a fairly hot property, especially with one of the chains in the area. I had originally planned to put it on the market by the middle of the year, getting everything lined up for an end-of-year takeover. Now I was staring at the fourth quarter and had done nothing.

"I suppose I need to get a business broker or run an ad in a magazine, like the one that brought Ed down to Green, but I'm just not sure," I said. "There's always so much going on, and I can't seem to focus on this. I know I need to."

"Are you having second thoughts?" Duke asked. "Because from the looks of things, you can pay on your line of credit and easily keep the paper, if you want to. I'd be happy to sit down with you and go over any of those numbers."

That, however, opened a door I was not about to walk through.

"No, of course not," I said. "I definitely plan to sell the paper. I just am not sure how I want to proceed. I want to get the best price I can, and I need to keep this quiet. I don't think it would be good for the staff or the town if they knew the paper was about to go on the block again."

I knew, too, that the sale of the paper would mean I had to make another big decision—what I was going to do with the rest of my life.

After lunch I immediately got on the phone with Marti. "Let's take a few days off and take a little vacation," I said. "I need a break."

We decided I would drive up to Ohio, stopping to see my brothers and spending a few days at Marti's place. We'd shop, eat at our favorite restaurants, and go to a new spa that a former reporter had opened. If a manicure and pedicure with my best friend didn't help me feel better, nothing would.

My friends in Green thought the vacation was a great idea. "You've been working too hard," Iris Jo said. "We can hold down the fort." "Check out the antiques up there," Rose said. "See what the prices are doing."

"You're chewing on something in that brain of yours, aren't you?" Aunt Helen asked. "Does this have to do with the sale of the paper?" Okay, maybe Helen didn't think the vacation was a great idea.

Ed's death was on my mind, too. Only a year earlier, he had been excited about moving to Green, making plans he would never have the opportunity to keep.

The unknown loomed, waiting to grab me around the throat. I found myself waking up in the middle of the night, restless and unable to go back to sleep. I snapped at people at work, including Katy when she turned her column in late.

"I'm *s-o-r-r-y,*" she said, drawing the word out to about four syllables. "It won't happen again."

"See that it doesn't," I said, and hurried back to my office.

The next afternoon, she stuck her head in and asked if I had a minute. "Are you mad at me?" she asked. "Did I do something wrong?"

"Oh, no, Katy," I said. "I'm so sorry. I just have a lot on my mind. I need to make some business decisions and to take care of a few things."

"Oh, you mean about selling the paper."

"What? What do you mean? Of course not. Business things."

"Everyone says you're trying to decide who to sell the paper to. That you had a year to get rid of it, and it's time."

In some way her remark made me love my little paper all the more. Rumors and speculation were the fuel that kept things going at newspapers across the country, and *The News-Item* was no different.

I looked Katy straight in the eyes and wondered how much to say. "I miss my friend Ed" were the words that came out. "This was supposed to be his paper, not mine. He was the one who was meant to move down here and do all these cool things and fight the battles and meet all of you and eat all those doughnuts."

Katy perched on the edge of a cabinet near the door, the place she usually chose to sit when she came to see me. "Maybe you should go see Pastor Jean. She's smart. She's usually pretty open-minded. I talk to her a lot."

She turned to walk out, and I fidgeted with papers on my desk.

"Lois?"

I looked up.

"You'll do the right thing."

After that conversation, I practically flew out of town, desperate to catch my breath, regain perspective, and reconnect with old friends and family. I packed up and left two days early, figuring I could stay a little longer, spoiling my nephews and niece. A book on tape did not keep my attention. My thoughts rolled. I finally pulled out a notebook and put it in the passenger seat, jotting to-do's for the next three or four months.

As the list took shape, a calmer feeling came. This I was good at—planning and setting goals. The right buyer was out there somewhere, ready for me to unload the paper. For a minute I thought about using one of *The News-Item*'s "three lines for three dollars" classified ads and laughed to myself.

Visiting cleared my mind. My noisy family told funny old stories, ones that we retold every time we were together. My brothers and their wives took me out to eat and listened to the highlights of life in Green. "You can't believe how hot and humid it is in the summer," I said. "I don't know how anyone can live there all their life."

The Dayton leg of the trip was bittersweet. Marti invited a lot of the old gang over to her place to play Scrabble, and I showed them a few editions of *The News-Item*.

"Look, here are young Katy's columns. She's good, don't you think?"

"I'm a fan of Katy's already," Marti said. "You've talked about her nonstop these past few months. I think we'll all be working for her one day."

I pulled out a funny story we had run about a policeman barking on the police radio. "No one would confess," I said, "and no one would rat on the guy. So, the entire department got written up. Only in Green." My former colleagues passed the story around. "You'll never believe where we got the tip. My elderly friend Helen called it in. One of her 'old lady friends,' as she calls them, listens to the scanner all day and all night. She called Helen to tell her someone was barking incessantly. Helen didn't believe her but promised to give me a call."

"You have got to be kidding," the Dayton cops reporter said. "Let me see that."

"When I mentioned it at the paper, one of the staff had heard it too. It turned into a great story. Look at those quotes. The police chief actually says, 'I had told them before they could not bark on the radio.'"

Everyone laughed.

"It's like I never left," I told Marti when our friends cleared out. "I honestly think I could walk in tomorrow, sit down at the city desk and people would think I had been on vacation for a few days."

Marti and her new boyfriend, Gary, took me out to eat. I liked the guy in spite of myself. He was funny, loved to read, and seemed to be a deep thinker without being pompous. He "felt the call to be a minister" in his late twenties, after a few years as an engineer.

"I kept thinking about spending the rest of my life in an office and how I wanted to use my time and energy," he said. "It was like something was nibbling at my soul, just wouldn't leave me alone. Then I took some kids to youth camp. I watched them learn about Christ. It's hard to describe, but something tugged at my heart. I knew I had to learn more and do something with it. Eventually I realized God was calling me to be a pastor."

He reached out and grabbed Marti's hand, held onto it. "But don't get me wrong; I sure don't think God wants everyone to be a preacher. I mean, if we were all preachers, who would we preach to?"

"Good point," I said, toasting him with my water glass.

"I really like the work Marti does," he said, squeezing her hand. "I think everybody has these fantastic gifts, and they're supposed to use them in ways that make them happy and that help the world be a better place. Like Marti. You, too, Lois. That's a big deal what you do. Telling stories. Keeping people informed."

He stopped and laughed again. "I'm preaching, aren't I? And I promised Marti I wouldn't do that."

Marti was crazy about him, and I figured I'd be back in Dayton within a year for a wedding. "You're probably not going to make our Mediterranean cruise when we turn forty, are you?" I asked her. "You'd better start using some of that new prayer power to help me find a man. Make up for abandoning me."

"Will do, sister. Will do."

As my visit wound down, I debated whether to go into the *Post* newsroom. "Most of the people who matter to me were at your party," I told Marti. "But I might work there again one day and need to stay connected."

"Go with your gut," she said.

In the end, the pull was too great. I stopped by late in the morning, right before people headed to lunch and before things got too hectic. I signed in at the front counter and stepped in the door to the sound of ringing phones and the police radio. One of the many TV sets blared. A scorched smell immediately told me the coffee pot was empty but no one had bothered to turn it off. The commotion momentarily overcame me.

The first person I saw was managing editor Diane, sitting in Ed's office. She jumped up and ran out to shake my hand. "Lois, how in the world are you? How's life down South?"

"Hey, Diane, good to see you. Things are good. How about with you?"

"Oh, busy as always. You know the drill. When you coming back to straighten out that city desk?"

A pang of regret ran straight through me. I could be sitting in her office. I could be running this newsroom. I pasted a smile on my face.

"Not sure, but don't forget about me," I said, wandering off while she was still talking.

Just when I was about to scoot out, Zach caught my eye and asked me if I had time for him to buy me a bite to eat. "I heard you were in town, and I need to talk to you."

I almost turned him down, but was curious and still had a little of that feeling that he was the boss. "You buying? Then, sure I have time for lunch," I said, wondering why I had come by the paper at all.

Predictably, we walked down the street to Buddy's and had a plate lunch. I did not feel nearly as nostalgic as I expected, and, after living in North Louisiana for nearly a year, the food didn't taste as good either. Near the end of the meal, Zach laid his napkin on the table and leaned over toward me, propped up on his elbows. "So, you've just about done your time down in *Lose-iana*, haven't you?" he asked, emphasizing the first syllable, as though making a joke.

"Yep, can't believe it. Been there almost a year. Time has gone so fast."

"You ready to come back to a real newspaper?"

"Well, last time I checked, my staff thought *The News-Item* was a real newspaper," I said, the veins in my forehead feeling as though they might explode. "It's actually a very real newspaper, and we're making money, too." Immediately I wished I did not sound so defensive.

He put up his hands, as though holding me back. "No offense intended. I'm sure it's a great little paper. But the company has a job they want you to consider, the top editor's job down in Asheville. The guy who's there is being promoted, and they're hoping you're ready to come back into the fold."

I was caught totally off guard. Asheville was a great city, and the *Asheville Advertiser* had done terrific work in the past couple of years, including being named one of the best small dailies in the country. This was one of those jobs that people who played the corporate-move game always put on their lists.

"I thought you were mad at me for leaving," I said. My move to Green had not pleased the powers that be.

Ed used to joke that this was a company that did not like breakups. "They can be ready to fire you," he said, "and they're still mad if you leave." I focused my attention back on Zach.

"Oh, we all hated to see you go," he said, "but everyone knew that Ed had left you in a real pickle. What were you going to do? But now the year's almost over, and we want you back. This is a good job, Lois, a great opportunity."

I could not immediately say no to this, any more than I could turn Zach down for lunch. "Let me think about it," I said. "What kind of timetable are we looking at?"

"They want to get someone in there within the next sixty days or so," he said. "Let's get you down there for an interview."

We walked back to the paper, talking logistics, and shook hands. Somehow our conversation had moved from my saying I would think about the job to planning to call Zach before I left Dayton to give him possible interview dates.

"I'll set things in motion," he said, "and get the publisher in Asheville to call you, follow up with a corporate call, get you some copies of the paper. You know the drill."

Maybe this was the sign I needed. My time in Green was wrapping up, and this would be a good job, a place that clearly said I was moving up in the chain. Marti and I had visited Asheville on vacation several years ago, and it was a beautiful town in a booming area. People bought vacation homes there, for heaven's sake, so it must be a good place to live. Things were falling into place. I would know the next step in my life when I left Green.

Marti, though, wasn't as excited about the job as I thought she would be. "It would be a good place to live," she said, "and the paper's good. But you know how corporate works. Do you really want that?"

"Marti, you know I have to do something. Plus, I'm getting tired of a tiny town in the middle of nowhere. You know we'd have fun if I were in North Carolina."

My preliminary talk with the publisher the next day went well. "I'll overnight you some papers and get my secretary to get you some flight options. I look forward to sitting down face-to-face," he said. "We know you've been running your own show down there in Louisiana. We'll keep that in mind as we work up your compensation package."

Marti and I both cried when I headed back to Green.

"You think long and hard before you jump back into this world," she said. "You seem happier than I've seen you in a long time. Something is going on with you. I can't quite put my finger on it, but something's definitely happening."

"Oh, you've been hanging out with the preacher

too much," I said, trying to make light of the moment. We gave each other another long, hard hug, and I headed back to Green.

Everyone was so happy to see me when I returned that I felt ashamed.

"Welcome home," they all said, most giving me the standard hug. "We sure missed you. How were things up north?" Tammy asked.

Fairly quickly I went to my desk and set up a meeting at the bank with Duke. By the end of the next afternoon, he had lined me up with Jim Mills, a business broker in Shreveport, a nice man with experience in media properties and eager to help.

"I handled the sale for the McCullers," he said. "I was sorry to hear about your friend. I'm sure this has been a terrible strain on you this past year."

His observation was wrong.

"Thanks, but it's worked out okay," I said. "This year has strangely enough been a good one. Lots of nice people, some interesting situations. It's not a bad little town."

I didn't mention that I liked myself better than I had a year ago.

"How long do you think this sale might take?" I asked. "Can we keep it super confidential?"

"No problem with keeping it quiet," he said. "And it should come together quickly. No guarantees, of course, but this should be a strong property. Sit back and wait. Just sit back and wait."

During the next few days, the Asheville job kept me tied up in knots. I knew *The News-Item* sale would work out. Some of Rose's optimism must have rubbed off on me. I was less sure about the path that lay beyond that.

A call from Marti brought it all pouring out. "The timing on all of this stinks," I said. "I want a job precisely at the end of the year. But if I walk away from Asheville, I'll probably be out of the company for good. Unless I'm willing to work night cops in Danville or Midland or something like that."

"You'll know," Marti said. "You always do."

When the package arrived with the copies of the *Advertiser*, I left early and took them home. As I looked through them, I found myself comparing what *The News-Item* had done, ideas we executed better than this much bigger staff. The paper was full of wire copy and did not give me a feel for the people who lived there. I knew I was looking for things to dislike, but I kept thinking, "This is one of the best little papers in the country?"

I went to wash the ink off my hands when I heard someone tapping lightly on my front door. "Lois, it's Jean, Jean Hours from the church up the road."

Her visit surprised me. She had not dropped by once since I had moved in, and she apologized for doing so tonight.

"I know people hate preachers who come calling at all hours of the day and night, interrupting, acting pushy." She laughed. "But I was headed into town to pick up some groceries, and I asked God to show me someone I could help . . . and you popped into my mind. I decided to drive down here and see if you were home."

She fidgeted with her car keys. "Am I crazy or incredibly intuitive?"

I sat down slowly in an old oak rocker and laughed sheepishly.

"I would say you've probably got intuition covered at the moment. I am struggling with a big decision. I guess God knew I needed some help."

15

"Neighbors out in the Pelican Place community are concerned about a remodeling project on the south side of town, converting the old Sears mail order center into Bud's Beer Barn. I hope you'll join me in complaining to Mr. Bud and seeing if we can't stop this before it goes too far."

—The Green News-Item

Katy was right.

Talking to Pastor Jean helped immensely.

"What next step feels best to you?" she asked. "What would you most like to do with your life?"

She was a good listener, one of those people who let you finish a thought before they jump in. She didn't throw out a lot of advice, but asked several questions that made me think in new ways. Mostly she encouraged me to believe in myself, to trust that I would make the right decision.

"It's tough sometimes to do what you're supposed to do. I know it's tough." She paused. "I'll admit it was plenty hard to give up my life as a teacher and a good retirement plan and go to seminary. And coming here was a bit of a shock."

"So," I asked. "Why did you really do it? Why not just keep your comfortable life in Baton Rouge?"

"Well, I did cry some, I'll admit. And I demanded that God tell me why he was leaving me out in the wilderness, apart from my husband. Sending me to this little country church where people often seemed more worried about getting out on time than about the sermon. But I knew that wherever I went, God would go with me. That's why I did it. God is with me."

She took a Kleenex out of her pocket and wiped her nose. "I sometimes over-think things. It is very hard for me to trust God completely with my life. Too often I believe I know better than he does."

"I know what you mean," I said. "I have to tell you that I don't trust God to help me know what to do. Ever since my mother died and then Ed, I figure I'm on my own—that I have to make decisions and be prepared for the consequences. I gave up on that whole faith thing—no offense—in my mid-twenties. Besides why would God be interested in my life when he's got the whole world to take care of? I'd say there are lots of things more important than my needy self."

My speech was blunter than I intended, and I took a deep breath before continuing. "Oh, that's not a hundred percent true. I didn't really throw my religion in God's face when my mother died. I let it shrivel from benign neglect. I was hurt and mad, and my life was busy. I kept looking in other directions, mostly work, and ignoring anything to do with God."

I shrugged. "My faith got smaller and smaller until it disappeared from my daily routine. No prayer. No Bible study. No church."

"Lois, I must tell you I believe God has great plans for your life, no matter how much doubt you have. I think God wants great things for you and that He plans for you to succeed."

She smiled. "When I look at you, I see so many gifts just waiting to burst out—like those gorgeous blooms on the hydrangeas at the parsonage. I didn't even know they were down in there, but they did. And when they shot out, they took my breath away. But, man, do those bushes take attention. I nearly let them die this summer, till I realized they need a little drink of water every evening."

The pastor's talk was inspiring. The hydrangea analogy was more poetic than Jean's usual matter-of-fact speech. Aunt Helen's hydrangeas awed me. When I arrived they were basically only sticks, but by early summer they were the most beautiful things I had ever seen. They did require time and attention every day.

"I'd like to think there is a grand plan for my life," I said, "that I was meant to do something special. I sure hope I have not been put on earth to flounder. But what am I supposed to do about Asheville? If God has this great purpose for me, what is it?"

"Well, I usually tell people their purpose in life is to love God and to love others, wherever they are and whatever they're doing and to make sure they're enjoying life along the way." She paused. "But something tells me that isn't going to be specific enough for you."

"I'm going to need more than that, Pastor."

"Take a tiny step and ask God for help. Listen for an answer. See what happens."

Her response wasn't an easy how-to list, but over the next few days, I did just that. I suddenly remembered asking for "help" in Dayton, not praying exactly but knowing I could not make the big decisions about the managing editor's job and moving to Green on my own. I recalled the rainbow and the voice telling me to "go." Had that been God trying to nudge me along or my own subconscious, knowing my life needed a change?

The weather had turned cooler, and fall was definitely coming. The light had shifted in the sky. I would get up early and sit in my porch swing and return there at the end of the day. I began each of these sessions, as I thought of them, by saying, "Help." And I sat and waited and listened.

Before long everything that happened was subject to scrutiny. Was this God talking? Was that? Or was this evil trying to lead me away? Was I on the right track? Who should I sell the paper to? Nothing was clear. I was confused and feeling a little crazy.

"Help," I said a hundred times a day. "Help, help, help."

Somewhat embarrassed, I called Pastor Jean and asked her if I could stop by on my way home from work. "I need help," I said. "This listening thing isn't working out for me, and I'm going nuts."

When I arrived late that afternoon, Jean was at the church, straightening hymnals in the sanctuary and picking up old bulletins.

"It's so much easier than writing a sermon," she said. "And it keeps me from getting too stuffy."

The sun looked different than it had the other times I had been in this building. It came in from another angle and was dimmer, a glow that softened everything. We sat on the front-row pew, each on one end. I started to say something, but Jean held up her hand and smiled.

"Listen," she said.

We sat there for fifteen minutes in silence. It was so quiet that I could hear the big old clock in the back of the church ticking. I heard a bug flying up to the light, making an odd buzzing noise. I heard Jean when she took a deep breath, as though she was cleansing her lungs. It was strange at first, and I fidgeted. Slowly I relaxed.

I took a deep breath and felt it flow throughout my body. I calmly looked at everything in front of me, as though I observed it through another person's eyes—the beautiful spider lilies on the altar, still fresh although they had been there several days, the handmade doily they sat on, a homemade banner that said, "My peace I leave with you."

Peace. I took another breath.

Jean saw me looking at the banner and spoke softly.

"That was made by the Hope Small Group for Iris Jo when Matt died. They wanted to do something more than just cook, and they came up with that idea. They did it in three days and gave it to her for the memorial service. It's been hanging here ever since. We all get a lot of comfort from it, and Iris Jo said it belongs here."

She read from the banner. " 'My peace I leave with you.' That's what you can call upon, Lois. Peace not as the world gives. Listen for God's peace. Watch for those red flags that tell you something isn't right, that you're going in the wrong direction. You're smart enough to see them. Notice when things feel right. Take things a step at a time, the best next step and the best next step and the next. When you're in doubt about something, don't do it. Wait for the peace."

She stopped. " 'My peace I leave with you. Peace not as the world gives. Do not let your hearts be troubled, and do not be afraid.' "

I took another deep breath and said, "Thanks."

"I just want to say one more thing. This peace goes beyond what we can understand. You can try all you want to fit it into some neat little package, but it won't go. God's greater than you are, understands more, loves more. God wants more for you than you have even begun to imagine." She stood up. "You ready for some supper?"

Jean and I had a great visit that night. She showed me pictures of her family and told me more about her move to Green. We ate a meal she had in the freezer. "It's one of the great perks of my job," she said. "I am fed incredibly well. In cities, people don't cook much anymore. You know, they bring Kentucky Fried Chicken or store-bought cookies. But here—all homemade. I've put on twenty pounds in just over a year, and I don't even care."

The next morning I went out and sat in my swing and said, "Help." Almost immediately I postponed my interview in Asheville.

"The time is not right for me to leave town again," I told the publisher. "Plus, I'm not ready to commit to another newspaper job just yet. I have many details to take care of with the paper I own."

Following the phone call, an immense sense of relief washed over me. I knew I had done the right thing. If they wouldn't wait to talk to me, I would have other opportunities, after *The News-Item* sold.

It was a good thing I hadn't gone. The week I would have left, Alex's story on the housing development finally came through. He had several great stories that implicated Major in a series of potentially illegal moves and had big-time scandal written all over it.

"Alex, you know we're just a little newspaper, and we are about to take on one of the most well-known men in North Louisiana," I said to the young reporter, both proud and scared. "You know that, right?"

"Lois, have a little faith in me," he said. "I've been working on this for months. I'm not going into it willy-nilly."

Demanding to know his sources and to see data, I regularly grilled Alex. Excited about what he had come up with, he was remarkably unflappable, only losing his cool a couple of times. "Basically, Lois," he said, clearly delighting in his news, "Major hired a friend's firm to do the environmental study on the first development, Mossy

Bend. His friend conveniently overlooked key problems, such as septic tanks emptying into the lake. The same firm was lined up to do the study on Cypress Point."

"And there's more?" I tapped my pencil on his desk, feeling a knot in my stomach.

"A memo from the state environmental office was ignored. It said plainly the Mossy Bend development was too close to the lake, opened up flooding and pollution issues. Gave it a no-go to be built." He fished around in a pile of papers on his desk. "The memo says, and I quote, 'It would be a travesty to build in the wetlands area and would do irreparable harm to the lake.'"

In addition, Major had been getting federal money to redo his rental houses in Lakeside, with the government paying exorbitant subsidies for shoddy work. The tenants were caught in the middle. Alex had taken pictures of the work, including electrical outlets with huge gaps around them, roofs that were patched, and basic carpentry that was clearly substandard. He had copies of invoices for the work, outrageous bills for small jobs. "The tenants told me they got government checks for the work and gave the money to one of Major's employees, getting to keep twenty dollars as a handling fee."

The man's greed and gall astounded me. The facts were so explosive I became extraordinarily cautious, reminding Alex not to talk with anyone

187

except Tom and me and to lock up his notes. He used the telephone in my office to interview sources, so no one could overhear.

"This is extremely sensitive," I said to Tammy and Iris Jo, "and we must not let it leak out until we are ready." I knew Major would not roll over when the stories appeared, that he would attack the paper and try to discredit us. My journalistic experience warred with my responsibilities as owner of the paper. I had visions of us being sued and losing everything, of Major sitting in my office, crowing that he had beaten me and taking over *The News-Item*. As a reporter, I had been annoyed when an editor or publisher wanted to lawyer my story, as they called it, but I wasn't about to let these go without letting a lawyer take a look at them.

Before I got that far, however, I got a call from Chuck McCuller, asking if he and Dub could come by and see me. I had heard occasionally from the Big Boys in the past six months or so, running into them at chamber meetings or getting a call when they didn't like something in the paper. This would only be their second visit.

Although the McCuller name had not come up in any of Alex's research, Marcus Taylor had mentioned them as partners in Major's real estate developments. I thought of Pastor Jean and her "red flags" and figured the call was not a social one.

They arrived early, and when I walked in, Chuck sat at my desk. Dub wandered around, flipping through a couple of files that lay on the little coffee table. They acted like they owned the place, and I realized how much had changed in less than a year. I shepherded them into the conference room, eager to get them out of my office.

"Miss Lois," Dub opened, "we appreciate all you've done with *The News-Item*. You've made some good changes, and we like the efforts you've made to revitalize downtown."

"But," Chuck continued, "we have heard some rather distressing news, and we think you should know about it. Folks are saying the newspaper is asking questions around town that it has no business asking."

I tried to look shocked. "Really? What kind of questions?"

Dub took up his part again. "People are saying that sloppy young reporter Alex is trying to dig up dirt on Major Wilson and some of the other business leaders in town, that he's out to get them and throwing around all sorts of allegations. False allegations, might I add? It's slanderous, and it's not good for the town. You'd better keep an eye on him because you might find yourself getting sued."

"Plus," Chuck said, "there's lots of advertisers involved, and you sure don't want them to cancel their advertising."

"You need to kill this story, this investigation, whatever it is," he continued. "You don't want this kid to tear down all the goodwill you've built up, and it's just not good for Green, dragging good people's names through the mud. Newspapers always have to be looking for the bad. Why can't you just leave well enough alone?"

Major must be about to have a stroke if he had sent Chuck and Dub over for this discussion.

"Are you referring to the stories Alex is working on about the developments on the lake?" I asked in a calm voice.

They nodded.

"And you're familiar with those developments? Partners, I believe, in those developments? So you know all about Major Wilson's business deals and what he's doing out there?"

Suddenly it dawned on them that I was turning the tables.

"Now wait just a minute," Chuck said, standing up so quickly that I thought he was going to turn over the chair. He leaned over the table with both hands spread out, holding him up. "We're partners with Major, sure. Everyone knows that. But we aren't involved in the daily workings of the business. Dub and I haven't done anything wrong, and you better watch what you say."

Watching the two men try to decide whether to cover their own hide or defend Major was one of the more interesting interactions I'd ever had in the news business. It was clear they were trying to size me up, to figure out how much I knew and what the paper was going to do.

Chuck was still standing, and slowly Dub stood up too.

"Kill the story or you'll regret it," Chuck said, and they stormed out.

We hired an attorney in Shreveport to look over the package. He had First Amendment experience, and I did not want anyone in Green to have an early look. My banker recommended "the young Walt King." He and his father had done work for the paper before, and Walt turned out to be exactly the lawyer we needed.

"You know, Alex," I said on our drive to Walt's office, "the thing about good newspaper lawyers is they never try to talk you out of running a story. They just try to let you know your likelihood of getting sued and of winning the case if you do get sued. Wonder what this one will say?"

"These are very interesting stories," Walt said, as he entered the law library where a secretary had parked us. "You've got some good stuff here."

Alex and I both probably loved him at that moment.

Walt was a short, bookish man in his mid-thirties, a look I found appealing. I was glad I had worn a sharp-looking suit and a nice pair of flats. He had a quick sense of humor and was methodical as we went through the stories. He made a few suggestions for Alex to follow up on and calmed my jumpy stomach.

"Don't hesitate to call," he said as we prepared to leave. "I'll do whatever I can for you. I'll be glad to come down to Green anytime you need me."

I had been hesitant to hire him because I wasn't sure we had enough money, but decided we probably couldn't afford not to hire him. When I asked about his rates, he said, "This one's on me and my Dad. You can pay for the next visit. I like what you're trying to do."

Every copy of the newspaper sold out when the Major Wilson stories broke.

Alex waited to get Major's response till a couple of days before they were to run. That had been my idea, and Walt agreed. As expected, Major refused to return Alex's calls, having Linda tell the reporter he was tied up. Finally Alex went to his office, and Major blew up. He ultimately provided a written statement, denying any wrongdoing. "I have lived in Green my entire life," he said. "I have served faithfully as a public servant and worked tirelessly to make this a better place to live. I am shocked and disappointed that the local newspaper has chosen to attack innocent people."

"Run the statement in its entirety on page one," Walt said, and we did.

The day before the first stories ran, Lee Roy came into my office, shut the door hard, and said,

"I hear we're doing an exposé on one of our most important advertisers. What are you trying to do, kill the paper?"

"No, Lee Roy, I'm trying to keep the paper alive."

He leaned over my desk, both hands gripping the edge. "This is some bogus setup, and you know it. You disliked Major from the minute you laid eyes on him. Just because he doesn't kowtow to you."

"Perhaps this would be the time for me to remind you that I own this newspaper, not you. These stories are an excellent example of the public service a true newspaper provides." I stood up and glared back at him. "Now, please get out of my office this minute."

I gasped when he left, knowing the stories would have a financial implication. If nothing else, just the loss of Major's real estate advertising would be a blow, and I knew we would lose his car dealer business for the short term.

The stories were picked up by the Associated Press wire and ran all over the state. Alex rushed into my office a few days later with a broad grin. "There's going to be a federal investigation of Major. The Cypress Point development is on indefinite hold."

While some people clearly believed the paper shouldn't make waves, most were supportive.

"It's about time someone dug around a little,"

Rose said. "People should be honest. It isn't right when people use their positions for personal gain." Others, such as Linda, weren't quite so sure. "Even though I don't necessarily like the man," she said, "I don't want harm to come to him."

"I'm with you, Linda," I said, surprised by the way I felt. "I like the stories we do about nice people doing positive things. Those make me feel really good." I took a deep breath. "This investigative work has been hard on all of us. But I know, too, it's *The News-Item*'s place to do it all—to talk about the good and shine light on the bad. It will make Green a better place to live."

One of the unintended consequences of the stories came the day after we broke the news of the impending federal investigation.

My attorney Walt King called and asked me on a date.

16

*Congratulations to Mr. Irman Jackson for
having the first bale of cotton ginned this
year in the parish. Mr. Irman was honored
with a plaque and received a standing
ovation at the gin.*

—*The Green News-Item*

Only a matter of weeks remained to do what I
wanted to do in Green. I knew the clock was running on my time here.

After the Major stories ran, I slowly reemerged,
needing to touch base with a dozen people. I made
a list that ranged from going to hear Jean preach
to following up with the Green Forward group to
see what we could do for the fall event. I set a
lunch meeting with Duke, a dinner date with Walt,
and a shopping trip with Kevin.

"I want to go antiquing with you and Linda," I
told Rose. "You and your Mom are invited to
lunch at the country club," I mentioned to Katy.
"Let's have brunch Saturday," I said to Aunt
Helen.

Iris Jo had invited me to a high school football
game, to see my neighbor Chris Craig and his
team in action, and I needed to do that before the
season ended. "Everyone in town goes to the

games," Iris Jo said. "Folks are wondering why you haven't gone to one." The weather was beautiful, and I kept trying to decide if I liked spring or fall in Louisiana better. The hickory trees turned bright yellow, and the vivid red sweet gums reminded me of Ohio. The cypresses on the lake became a rusty red color. "They're almost exactly the color of your hair," I told Iris Jo, and she smiled that warm smile of hers.

The terribly hot weather was definitely gone, and people seemed to have a little more pep in their step.

With fall also came the special election to fill the retiring mayor's seat. The news staff gathered for lunch at the country club as a thank-you for everyone's hard work, and I mentioned the upcoming primary.

"Now that I've thanked you," I said, "we need to plan something bigger and better with the upcoming election."

They all groaned at first. They were tired, and things had been tense around town as the Major Wilson stories continued to break. Alex seemed a little ticked that I expected him to help with a new project so soon, and I turned to him. "I just don't feel like we have any choice. Thanks to you, we've raised the bar on what people expect from *The News-Item.* We have to keep on exceeding those expectations."

"Let's do an editorial campaign to get people

registered and motivated to vote," Tom said. "In our last election, we had twelve percent of the registered voters show up. Twelve percent! That's a crying shame."

Katy, who had gotten permission to check out of school for the luncheon and who was now getting journalism course credit for her work at *The News-Item*, wanted us to do something with young voters and even kids who couldn't vote.

"They're the future," she said. "We ought to ask them what they want in a mayor."

Alex couldn't keep pouting and threw out his idea—that we run photographs and blurbs on everyone considering running for mayor. One of the first names that surfaced on the potential candidates list was Eva Hillburn's. I had not thought of her as a politician, but it made perfect sense. I volunteered to call her.

"It's true," she said when I phoned later that day. "I'm thinking about running. I've been sitting on the sidelines for a long time. But I need to talk to you first."

"Me? Why? I'm not running," I said, joking.

"Thank goodness," she said. "You'd be a tough opponent. But seriously, I need to talk to you about some downtown business before I make my final decision."

We set up a supper meeting for the next night, hamburger buffet night at the country club. Maybe it was my imagination, but the place seemed totally different since my first meeting there with Eva. The Methodist preacher was there with his family. Kevin and her parents and a handful of African Americans I recognized from the neighborhood association were there. I knew about half the other people and spent ten minutes walking around the room visiting.

Eva shook my hand when she came in and quietly thanked me for our series on her brother. "You nailed down something I never could," she said. "Excellent work, even though it stung. I knew he was doing something illegal, but I couldn't figure out what it was. I'm so angry at him for abusing people's trust . . . and ashamed, too."

As we ate, we chatted about what was going on in town, the one-day OktoberFest planned for downtown and even a little bit about my vacation trip to Dayton. "So, are you thinking of moving back there?" she asked.

That question surprised me, but the answer was easy. "Oh, no, no, no. In fact, I probably need to go ahead and put my condo on the market. My renter's moving out in a couple of months."

"What are your plans?"

"To tell you the truth, they're up in the air right now. I'm still trying to recover from Alex's stories on Major and trying to get us all set for covering the mayor's race. You planning to run?" I wanted to turn the conversation back to her as quickly as possible, still not ready to discuss the sale of the paper.

"Well, that depends on you," she said. "I'm going to run unless you'll sell me *The News-Item*."

I set down my glass of tea so hard that it sloshed out on the white tablecloth.

"What?"

"I've been thinking about this a lot. I've always thought I might run for office, and the timing seems right with Oscar stepping down. It might be a little better if my brother weren't likely headed for jail, but people will get over that." She casually dipped a French fry into her catsup.

"I had just about decided for sure when I began to hear some talk that you're putting *The News-Item* on the market. I think I could have some fun with the paper, make a difference. It would have to be easier than walking door-to-door and kissing babies to get elected to office. Besides, I don't want just any owner coming in and taking over. You've shown us what a great owner can do. You've done more with that paper in a year than the McCullers did in a decade. So, is it for sale?"

A strange possessiveness about the paper moved across me, like it was mine and no way was Eva going to get her hands on it. That was ridiculous, since it was officially on the market. Someone would be getting it. I liked and respected Eva. She might be the perfect owner.

"I'm thinking about selling it, but I'd appreciate it if you kept that between us for right now. I've got to make hard decisions between now and the end of the year, and I don't want the staff to feel like the rug's getting pulled out from under them."

"I don't want to be too pushy, but have you listed it with a broker? I'd like to know some of the particulars. I have to make a decision quickly. If I'm going to run, I have to get a campaign organized right away."

I don't know why, but I could not tell Eva I had officially listed the newspaper. "Well, I have been talking to someone, but nothing's certain yet." Perilously close to lying, I felt bad. "I should know something for sure in a week or two."

Eva knew I wasn't totally upfront with her. She was all business when she reached out and touched my hand. "If you're selling it, I want a shot at it. But I have to know something soon."

Heading to my car, I wondered yet again how my life had gotten so complicated.

The next person I was to question about the mayor's post was Rose. Her name came up as a potential candidate because of her involvement with the downtown group. She quickly shot that down.

"Are you kidding me? I'd have to give up my mail job, and I'd probably lose all my business at the Holey Moley, and I'm not any kind of a politician." She paused for just a second. "But I have been thinking about getting involved in some-body's campaign. All the stuff you got us to do downtown and all that mess with Major. Good people have got to get involved."

Rose was much more excited, though, talking about my upcoming date with Walt. "I can't believe it. Finally. I've been trying to fix you up since the day I met you. I just don't understand how a woman can live alone, way out in the country."

"Rose, it's not like there's a trainload of eligible men in Green. I've met approximately three single men—one is eighty, the other's going through a vicious divorce and that Chris Craig guy hasn't even looked my way. Besides I haven't been here that long."

"Now, what are you going to wear? And what's he look like? Is he good-looking? What are y'all going to do, go out to eat, catch a movie?"

I laughed and went through her list. "I haven't thought about what I'm wearing. Something I've got in my closet. We're going to that seafood restaurant on the lake. He's nice enough looking, although he's a little short."

"Wear those black pants with that black-and-white shirt—that flowy one. And be sure to get your nails done. You're an attractive woman, and it's high time you found someone in your life."

I despised dating, but I had to admit being excited about going out for the first time in a year.

When you get to your thirties and haven't married, you've probably been out with at least two dozen men who were either weird, rude, boring, or a combination of the three. I felt optimistic about Walt.

We met for Sunday brunch at the nicest restaurant in the area, Brocato's Marina Inn. I suggested we go early, to beat the church crowd, and then worried that Walt was part of the church crowd.

"I go on Saturday," he said. "My church is very laid-back. My mother calls it rock-and-roll church."

He was already at the restaurant when I arrived and led me to our table, which had a beautiful view of the lake. Several people we knew came in and stopped at our table to chat. Walt had worked with some of them on cases down our way, and I recognized others from the community.

Everyone wanted to know how we met and how long we had known each other. We both were vague, implying that someone in town had introduced us, which was technically true since Duke had referred me to Walt. For the second time in two days I was deliberately misleading.

The date would have been more fun if I had not been mulling over what to do about Eva's interest in the newspaper. I had thought of little else since our supper. I had listed the paper with a broker. Eva's timetable put pressure on me to move faster than I wanted. It could open up the Asheville job again.

"Don't you think?"

Walt was talking to me, and I had no idea what he had said. "I'm so sorry," I said, trying to make a joke of it. "I have had a lot on my mind. I think I must have zoned out there."

"You mentioned you haven't made it over to Dallas yet, and I was saying it might be fun to go over one weekend, see some movies and eat out. We could go and come in one day if we got an early start."

"That does sound like fun," I said. But I had few weekends left in Green and wasn't sure I wanted to give them up for an excursion to Texas. "There's a lot going on, though, so I'll just have to see."

I'd put a damper on Walt's enthusiasm, but the rest of our date was enjoyable. I took him over to the paper for a tour.

"It's been years since I was in here," he said. "This is great. I don't remember the press being so big."

"Do you remember the newsroom being this cluttered?" I asked.

"Absolutely," he said.

We parted in the parking lot with a quick hug, no kiss. I headed home, longing for some of that peace that Pastor Jean had told me about.

I opened the door and the phone rang.

"Lois? It's Iris Jo. Aunt Helen took a fall and is in the hospital. I knew you would want to know."

"Up in Shreveport or the little Green clinic?"

"She's here. They think they'll discharge her tomorrow, but they want to keep an eye on her."

I hurried to the clinic, worried. When I walked into her room, Helen was alone and looked pale and much more fragile than usual. I patted her hand. "So you took a tumble, huh? How are you doing?"

"I've had better days," she said. "But I've also had worse." Aunt Helen was always looking at things from a different point of view. "How about you?"

I wanted to talk about Eva's interest in the newspaper, but I knew the time wasn't right, so I went for the other high-interest topic.

"I had a date today."

"Today?" I had gotten her attention. "Not some lowlife, I hope?"

"No, ma'am, a lawyer from up in Shreveport. Nice guy. Walt King."

"Oh, young Walt," she said. "I know him. Know his daddy quite well. Used to do some work for the paper. He's done lots of legal work for me over the years. Nearly married him when I was a young woman."

Helen rarely said anything about her love life. She had never married but had been engaged to a guy who was killed in some sort of farming accident. I was surprised when she continued. "Most people think that Joe Hudson was the love of my life, and that I never married because he got killed. Truth is, Lois, Walt senior was my true love, and darned if he didn't break up with me and marry someone else. Nice gal, too, but I still don't know what she had on me."

Maybe Helen was on more pain medication than I realized. I patted her hand again. "Well, if he's anything like his son, he's a nice man," I said. "But he must not be too smart if he let you get away."

"You think this will amount to anything?"

"Oh, who knows? I sort of doubt it. He's a nice guy, but I'm not a Louisiana girl."

"So it's true, huh? You are planning to sell the paper."

I will never cease to be amazed at how news travels. When people ask to tell me something off-the-record, I want to laugh. A thousand people probably already know it, or will by the time the day is out. "I'm thinking about it, Aunt Helen. That's been the plan all along. What do you think?"

"Dumbest idea I ever heard. You were made to run this paper. You've been better to this place than anything that's happened in years. I can't even believe you'd ask me about it."

I pulled my chair up closer to her bed.

"It's always been the plan," I repeated. "You know the terms of the deal. This paper wasn't cheap, and there's a hefty note over at the bank with my name on it. I need to take care of that."

"Oh, that's baloney. It isn't the money, and you know it. You're a smart girl, and you could pay that line of credit and take out more and keep it going. You know how that game works. That paper makes good money, too. You're just running away."

I had been subjected to these kinds of tirades from Helen before, and I knew she didn't feel good. I should probably coddle her.

"Running away? Running away? Just what is it that I'm supposed to be running away from?" I decided I didn't want to coddle her.

"From life, girl," she said, more gently. "From life. You've made more friends in Green in less than a year than lots of people make their whole life. You've helped change this place for the better, and you know it. But you're afraid of letting anyone get too close to you, to commit to sticking around. You're half scared of failing at the paper, somehow getting deep into debt and not being able to get out. And you're running from God."

"Running from God? I am not running from God. What in the world are you talking about?"

I was getting increasingly louder, and an aide stuck her head in the door. I lowered my voice. "I am not running from God or from my friends or from anyone. Except I may run from you if you keep at me. Aren't I supposed to be giving you a sponge bath, or something?"

"No sponge baths, no chicken broth, and no bedpans," she said. "But you are running from

God. I'll tell you one thing—you're going to Nineveh whether you like it or not. So, you can go with good humor or you can keep running. God has a use for you, Miss Lois Barker, and you will not escape, no matter how hard and fast you run."

I looked at her, wondering for a moment if she was losing it. "Nineveh?"

"Yes, Nineveh—where God told Jonah to go. He ran and ran and landed in the belly of a whale and still wound up in Nineveh. One way or another, you're going to Nineveh."

17

"Thank you to my neighbors in the Caroline community who sent me recipes to share with my faithful readers. After nearly a decade of laying the groundwork for this coup, Sarah Johnson pried her mother's amazing turnip green recipe out of her. She calls them the world's finest turnip greens because they are. 'Just serve them with a hot pan of cornbread—and don't expect any leftovers.'"

—*The Green News-Item*

On my third date with Walt, I figured out how Lee Roy was stealing from the paper.

I made a picnic lunch for us, and we went out to the state park on one of those beautiful Louisiana autumn days that I had fallen in love with. We were eating sandwiches and talking when a flashy boat came by at high speed, with people yelling and laughing. I noticed an older man in an aluminum fishing boat shaking his head as the big boat's wake rocked him back and forth.

"What kind of an idiot goes that fast when people are close by?" I asked.

"A rich one, I'd say," Walt said. "That's a pretty expensive toy right there."

As the boat circled around, I noticed none other than Lee Roy Hicks himself at the wheel. "That's Lee Roy. Now how does he afford that boat on his salary?" I said, asking myself as much as Walt. Lee Roy was well paid by Green standards, but hardly made enough money to support his lifestyle, now that I thought about it. He lived in a fancy house out at Mossy Bend, drove a very nice car, and was always dressed in expensive, name-brand clothes. I had wondered how many of those fancy golf shirts he owned.

Suddenly an advertisement from the Friday paper popped into my mind, a full-page color ad for Lowrey Marine, a big regional boat dealer. Lee Roy had been ecstatic when the contract on Lowrey's came through. "The Lowreys are going to be great customers," he said, smiling more than I had seen him smile in months. "I've been trying to get their business for years."

But when I had looked at the financials for that

day's paper, the revenue from Lowrey's was low. I asked Lee Roy about it, and he gave me a complicated story about how they signed a contract and would pay higher rates later on. "I wanted to hook them good, so I worked with them on the front end," he said. "They're going to add at least twenty grand to our bottom line this next year."

Suddenly some of the gaps in the numbers came together for me. Had Lee Roy cut better deals for certain advertisers, giving himself a percentage along the way? He was well liked by many of the businesspeople in town, a loud, friendly guy who dressed well and loved to tell a good joke. He was very close to Major Wilson and the McCullers and had not forgiven me yet for the stories we were running and never missed an opportunity to complain about the newsroom.

He didn't like me, and I had been especially suspicious of him since Aunt Helen had suggested he might be stealing. But I could never put it all together.

Resisting the urge to hop up and rush to the paper, I tried to focus on Walt. With a complex theft scheme unwinding in my brain, that was difficult.

Even though we had been out several times, I had not invited Walt to my house yet. The drive out to Route 2 made his trip down to Green even longer, and keeping him in town kept him at arm's length. Meeting in the newspaper parking lot was easy.

He seemed surprised and a little hurt, though, when I wrapped up our date early and asked him to take me back to work. "I'm sorry, Walt, but I just have so much going on. I need to go over some records at the paper and take care of a few things." As soon as he drove off, I ran into my office and started digging through files. The clues were pretty obvious. I couldn't believe I hadn't picked up on this before.

I called Iris Jo. "I'm so sorry for bothering you at home on a weekend, but is there any way you can come to work for a while?" This was a woman who had worked for the Big Boys for years, so she didn't seem surprised at all by my request. When she arrived, I was practically dancing around my office, in excitement, anger, and nervousness.

"You sell the paper?" she asked in a somber tone.

"What? No, no, no," I said. Sooner rather than later I was going to have to come clean with all of these people who cared about this paper, this town, and me. "It's something else, something big. I need you to promise me you won't mention it to anyone, not anyone. Promise me."

"I promise. You know I don't talk about the paper's business, Lois," she said, sounding a little hurt.

She was right. She wouldn't tell any of my secrets. She was loyal, honest, and she liked me. "I know, and I'm sorry if I implied otherwise. I'd trust you with my life, but I'm not sure what we're going to find out."

By now she was totally confused.

"Have you ever wondered if Lee Roy was stealing from the paper?"

Her eyes got big, and she hesitated. "A time or two. But I never could pinpoint it. Why?"

I outlined my theory to her.

"That makes sense in a weird way," she said. "I can see where he might not mind taking money from you since it's pretty clear he doesn't like you. But he's tight with Chuck and Dub. Do you think this started when they were still here?"

"I'm not sure. I need your help to put it all together." For the next six hours we pulled invoices for advertisers and compared them to ads that had run in the newspaper for the past six months or so. Consistently we found ads that did not jibe with their bills. As I had expected, the primary recipient of Lee Roy's special ad rates was Major and his real estate business and car dealership. On the other hand, Eva always paid top rate, and her bills coincided perfectly with what she ran.

The amount of money the newspaper had been shorted was considerable.

"If this doesn't beat anything I've ever seen," Iris Jo said, running her hands through her hair. "I should have picked up on this. I am so sorry. I could have saved you a lot of money. This was my job, and I didn't catch it."

"Don't beat yourself up, Iris. You had no concrete evidence Lee Roy was stealing, and he chose a pretty slick way to do it. How could you notice money was missing if it never came to the books in the first place?"

"What are we going to do?" I liked the way she said "we" instead of "you." I knew she would back me up, no matter how much fur might fly.

"Well, we're going to act like nothing is going on, that we're cleaning out old files. If you're up to it, tomorrow afternoon we'll look at some more back editions and try to figure out when this started. Then I'll probably need to talk to Duke and to Walt, see how to proceed legally."

Before we headed home, we grabbed a quick bite to eat at the Cotton Boll and tried to chitchat, but neither of us could quit thinking about Lee Roy, the missing money and the challenges ahead. As we parted, Iris Jo gave me a hug. "You know you're welcome at church tomorrow if you want to come. We'd love to have you."

"Thanks," I said and climbed into my car, exhausted and wired.

When I got home, there was a medium-sized dog lying on my front porch. Cautiously climbing out of the car, I headed for the back door. The dog growled and whined and its tail thumped the porch. I looked closer, trying to figure out what was going on. It looked like one of Chris Craig's dogs . . . Kramer, was it? No,

Kramer was the big, lean dog. Mannix? Yes, that was it. Mannix.

"Hey, fellow, it's okay. You're Mannix, aren't you?" I tried to soothe the dog without getting too close. "It's okay. What's wrong with you, big guy? Are you hurt?"

The dog didn't get up when I walked around and into the house, instead giving a halfhearted bark and a whimper. I, on the other hand, let out a loud sigh. This was just what I needed tonight. Digging around for the tiny Green phonebook, I found the coach's number and dialed it, only to get no answer. I walked to the front of the house and used the screen door as a barrier between the dog and me, just in case he decided to bite. He whimpered again, gave a short growl and put his head down. His tail was still wagging, and I thought that was a good sign.

I dug out my emergency flashlight and shone it on him. Sure enough, there was a big smear of blood on his back, and his fur was matted where it had soaked through and dried. I had no idea what to do. I was deathly afraid of dogs, worn out, did not know how to go about getting this one treated, and was certain that my top-ranked employee was stealing me blind.

Desperate, I looked up a veterinary clinic in town and called. They suggested I carry the animal to my car and bring him in for a check up.

I put a towel in the back seat and nervously

approached the dog. "Easy, Mannix. I'm going to help you, buddy." The dog whimpered, but did not growl. I gingerly picked him up and carried him to the car. When I laid him down on the seat, he growled, but it was feeble and not very threatening.

I drove by Chris's house, hoping he would have come home, but the place was dark. I even turned around and drove back by a couple of his ponds, but didn't see him.

A nice young woman answered the night bell at the animal clinic and came out to help me carry Mannix. A quick check showed the dog had a deep laceration on his back. "I'm not sure if he's been hit by a car or gotten hung on something sharp," she said. "It'll require a closer look. He definitely needs stitches, but I don't think we'll have to do surgery."

I signed the paperwork, hoping I was doing the right thing. I noticed people out in the country were crazy about their dogs—but treated them differently than city people treated theirs. They let them run around in the yard, and they didn't seem to baby them so much. What if Chris thought that taking his dog to the vet was a stupid idea?

When they took the dog back to the treatment area, I called Chris again and again, using the phone on the sign-in counter. Finally, I tried Iris Jo and told her what had happened.

"He just left here frantic about Mannix," she said. "He'll be so relieved. I'll let him know."

Fifteen minutes later, Chris rushed into the clinic, and I quickly updated him. He came across the waiting room and gave me a big, tight hug. "Thank you so much, Lois. I don't know how I can ever repay you. Thank you. He's probably sort of a dumb mutt to you, but I love that animal, really all three of them. I didn't think he could get out of that fence. I feel terrible."

"Well, I think I'll head on back home. I'm glad everything worked out."

He stood up and hugged me again. That man could hug. He was a big, tall guy, sort of a forty-year-old version of the young athletes he worked with. "I owe you big time. I'll buy you dinner or something soon."

"You don't owe me, Chris. That's what neighbors do for each other. And besides you cleaned up my yard and didn't even take credit for it."

I opened the clinic door. "Well, I guess I do have one favor to ask. Stop by or give me a call in the next few days and let me know how Mannix is doing."

Driving home, I didn't feel quite so tired. I felt good about tackling my fears and getting the dog to the vet. Truthfully, I was somewhat touched by Chris's gratitude and the two warm hugs. Maybe this was a guy I could be friends with, since he lived just down the road. Of course, I wouldn't be here much longer, but maybe we could stay in touch.

I thought of him again just before I fell asleep and wondered what his wife had been like.

The next morning I overslept and woke up with that weird feeling where you know something is wrong but can't quite remember what it is.

Immediately it hit me.

I had uncovered Lee Roy's illegal actions at the newspaper and had to deal with them. No way could I leave that for the new owner. That brought to mind other topics always hovering near the surface of my brain—Eva's interest in the paper and the Asheville job. If I didn't give Eva a shot at *The News-Item*, I'd be cheating her in a way—and possibly even the people of Green. She knew how to run things and make money. But wouldn't she also make a great mayor? What if I kept dragging my heels on Asheville? They were impatient already.

"We've gone back to our other candidates," the publisher had e-mailed me the previous week. "Let us know if your timetable changes."

Getting out of bed, my first cup of coffee in hand, I called Aunt Helen. She had not seemed herself since her short stay in the hospital, and I made an effort to talk to her every day or so. When I tried her room, no one answered, so I called the nurse's station to leave a message.

"Oh, Lois, she asked us to call you, but we haven't had a minute. Helen was taken to the hospital again this morning. She had some shortness of breath."

When I got to the clinic, she had already been moved to a room, but she looked much worse than when last I had seen her. She was on oxygen, and her color was bad. My mother would have said she looked peaked.

For just a moment when I entered the room, I thought she didn't know me, but she quickly roused and greeted me. "You'd do anything to get out of going to church, wouldn't you?" she said.

"So would you apparently," I replied, leaning over to give her a quick kiss on the forehead. "You got a crush on the ER doc or something?"

"You journalists, can't get anything past you, can I?"

"So what's wrong with you?"

"Well, I'm eighty-three years old, a coot, and I seem to have some sort of problem with my heart. Apparently the home's fish sticks and French fries menu choice did not agree with me. What's wrong with you?"

"I'm thirty-six years old, never been married, own a newspaper I don't know what to do with, and have no idea what to do with my life. And right now fish sticks and French fries sound pretty good to me. Since you're doing so well, I think I'll run down to the cafeteria and see what they're serving for breakfast." I was hungry and out of sorts.

Aunt Helen was asleep when I returned, and at first it scared me. I thought she had died while I was eating bacon and eggs. I leaned over to see if she was breathing.

"Boo," she said right in my ear, in that deep, wavering voice I had first heard on the telephone in my office. I jumped and squeaked.

"You thought I had croaked, didn't you?"

I hung my head, a little embarrassed.

"I was just taking a catnap. Come sit over here." She patted the edge of the bed and moved over to make room for me to sit. I could tell Helen was tired, but it was clear she had something on her mind.

"Child, can I give you some advice about that newspaper?"

"Sure," I said, knowing she would give it to me one way or the other.

"Hang onto it. Be a good steward of it, the way you have been. Don't squander your gifts. Expect good things—great things—to happen. Have some fun. God has great plans for you."

And then she drifted off again.

Over the next few days, Aunt Helen's condition deteriorated quickly. They considered moving her up to Shreveport to an intensive care unit, but decided it was too risky. She had apparently suffered a mild heart attack and developed pneumonia, which she couldn't seem to shake.

She was seldom completely conscious, although I often thought she knew that I and a bevy of others were in the room. Young women from church came by to talk about lessons she had taught them, and older women told great stories about her friendship and crazy things she had done through the years. I sat with her for hours, hoping my presence would reassure her. She had gone downhill so quickly, joking with me and giving me advice one minute and lapsing into a coma-like state the next.

One afternoon Walt and his father came to see her. If Walt senior's presence didn't wake her up, nothing would.

Walt and I chatted quietly in the hall, leaving his dad with Helen. I figured some message might need to pass between them.

"I'm sorry I haven't returned your calls," I told Walt. "I've been trying to spend as much time up here as I can, and by the time I get home, I'm just pooped and it's late."

He put his arm around my shoulders. "It's okay, really. I understand. The way you treat Aunt Helen is one of the many reasons I'm crazy about you."

I was startled. I knew he liked me, but we had kept our relationship pretty much on the surface.

I changed the subject. "I've got a problem at the newspaper. I need to talk with you about it." I looked around to make sure no one could hear. "I haven't gotten all my ducks in a row yet, but I know someone's stealing from me. I'm going to need your legal help again."

"No problem. We can tackle that as soon as you

are ready. But you be careful, okay? People get a little crazy when someone backs them into a corner."

Suddenly there was a great commotion, and nurses rushed into Helen's room. She had died with the love of her life at her bedside, ironic since they had been apart for sixty years.

The doctor ultimately said her heart was weak, but I knew that wasn't the case. She was one of the biggest-, strongest-hearted people I had ever known.

I wish I could have had her in my life longer.

18

The Bouef Parish Sheriff's Department is holding two Jersey cows and a donkey found wandering on the old Route 2 cutoff. To claim the livestock, identify them and be prepared to pay the loose animal fine.

—The Green News-Item

The police came to the building to arrest Lee Roy. He cursed as he was led out. "You'll pay for this, Lois Barker. The McCullers will have your hide."

Once the district attorney talked about prison, however, Lee Roy wasted no time in laying the blame on the shoulders of the newspaper's former owners. He insisted Dub and Chuck had been siphoning money from the paper for years, had not paid taxes on it, and had not told their two siblings and Aunt Helen, who shared ownership of the paper. He was adamant they had helped him with his scam and taken a rather large cut.

With that much to go on, Iris Jo and I renewed our efforts, spending long hours at the office. The ordeal of gathering evidence for a criminal case and firing Lee Roy made my stomach churn. Knowing the Big Boys had likely been involved was even worse. The McCullers had been much more sophisticated in their schemes, but theft was not hard to find once we knew where to look.

"Looks to me like they were doing some of the same deals," Iris Jo said. "They took money from advertisers and didn't report it to their co-owners or the IRS. They overcharged the paper for years for expenses, used a separate account where money flowed from the printing business. That's a side business, you know, so it would be hard to see. They always took care of those books."

The revelations made me incredibly angry.

"The thing that makes me maddest," I said, "is that Dub and Chuck doctored the books between the time Ed made his offer and the time he was to take ownership of the paper. They took thousands of dollars out of the newspaper's accounts and into their own pockets, cheating my friend."

My voice cracked. "Ed was a good, decent man. He saved for years to buy this paper, and he didn't deserve the way they treated him. I hope they rot in jail."

Iris Jo was, as usual, calmer. "Your friend was a nice man. I enjoyed the couple of meetings I had with him and the phone conversations. I didn't know him very well, but I know one thing—he wouldn't want you to get bitter over this. Everything will work out. We're doing our part. Beyond that, you just have to let it go. Turn it over to God and hope that justice is done."

"I don't want to turn it over to God. I want a big fat case to turn over to a federal judge." I glanced at Iris Jo and knew she was acting as a friend. "Well, the federal judge probably thinks he's God anyway."

I leaned over and patted her arm. "Thanks for being such a great person, Iris Jo."

Through all of this, other friends came to see me, brought me food and generally cheered me up, knowing I was reeling from Helen's death and the pain of Lee Roy's deceit. Many had known Aunt Helen longer and maybe loved her more, but she added something special to my life. Her words would guide me long after she was gone.

The Big Boys were cool to me at the service, unaware of what I had in store for them. "We won't block your request to say a few words," Dub said, "but that doesn't mean we like it. We just don't want to be the ones causing a scene."

They were still angry that I had exposed Major's

dealings and furious at what I had done to their pal Lee Roy. They continued to maintain their ignorance about the inner workings of Major's business and Lee Roy's thefts. I figured they thought letting me speak at the funeral would solidify their innocence with the community.

The other McCuller siblings, a brother and two sisters who lived in Tennessee and Florida, were cordial and thanked me for being a friend to Aunt Helen and for continuing the traditions of *The News-Item*. They had clearly long since lost interest in the paper, if they had had any in the first place.

One of my best encouragers during these days was young Katy. She was outraged at any hint of wrongdoing in the world and had recently latched onto the idea of being a crusader. She said the sweetest things about my courage and reminded me several times a week not to give up.

"I'm praying for you," she said once. "That you'll have the strength to see this through and to keep working for good."

She was the most fascinating mix of grown-up and teenager, sometimes blowing me away with her wisdom and other times cracking me up with a silly discussion she was in at school. I hoped it might work out somewhere years down the line that Katy could own *The News-Item*. She was blossoming into a fine young woman and was going to make a magnificent journalist.

My neighbor Chris called a couple of times to update me on Mannix's recovery and to see how I was doing. He was effusive in thanking me for helping Mannix, and I could tell he was worried about how things were going at the paper.

"You be careful, okay?" he said.

Others, like Rose, Linda, and the Taylors, never let more than a few days go by without checking on me.

Kevin e-mailed every day and left numerous messages for me. "I am determined to cheer you up," she said when I called her back. "Phone tag gets old quick. I'm taking you to supper tomorrow, like it or not."

She strolled into the country club as though she had been a member for life, gracefully walking over to our table. She definitely belonged.

"Ready for a standing girls' night out?" she asked, plopping her huge purse onto a spare chair. "Because you're not leaving here without setting up dinner next month, restaurant of your choice."

"That's the kind of friend I love," I said. "Plans the next meal before we've even ordered this one. No wonder my jeans are getting tight."

After the club's famous turtle cheesecake, Kevin rummaged in her purse and pulled out photographs of her neighborhood. "Look at this mess. I wish my favorite muckraker could do something about the Lakeside Annex."

I flipped through the photos. "These remind me of my first moments in Green. I nearly turned around and left town. But your cottage looks so cute. It brightens the entire block."

We parted with plans to meet again for supper and to work on Kevin's neighborhood.

Even Pastor Jean called regularly and stopped by my house once in awhile. "I owe you big time," she said, sitting on my porch one evening. "All your news distracted folks from the lady preacher. Now if you could just get them to tithe."

Her visit lifted my spirits considerably.

"I'm better at what goes in the paper than what goes in the offering plate," I said. "But I can assemble something on a dinner plate. Want a bite to eat?"

The Green Forward group marched on without my presence at the meetings, pulling off a fun Saturday Oktoberfest. The high school band played, a civic club sold sausages on a stick, and churches organized games for children. Satisfaction rolled over me as I looked at the traffic outside my office window.

I needed the reassurance. I spent most of my time meeting with civil attorneys and criminal prosecutors, bankers, insurance company representatives, and people from every agency from the IRS to the FBI.

"Let's walk through this again," the district attorney said during what had become a typical afternoon meeting. "When did you first suspect someone stole from the paper?"

"She's told you this a dozen times already," Walt said. He rubbed the back of his neck as he spoke. "We've been over this very thing every day for a week. Not to mention having the same conversation with the assistant U.S. attorney in Alexandria."

"You know the grand jury's looking into the allegations," the D.A. said. "We've got malfeasance at the paper and Major's illegal activities. There's a lot riding on this."

"Let's get on with it," I said. "I'll do whatever it takes to make this right."

The IRS audit team showed up at the paper first thing one morning. "We'll need to go over your books from the past three years for starters," the agent said. "We'll let you know if we need more."

"But most of those records have already been subpoenaed in the criminal cases," Iris Jo said. "Can't this wait until those are resolved?"

"No ma'am, sure can't," one accountant said. "We must verify the accuracy of *The News-Item*'s tax returns for the past few years. See if proper taxes were paid."

"You mean the paper might owe taxes on money that was stolen?" I asked. "I'd better get Walt on the phone."

The McCullers put out a statement defending their good name as the news unfolded. "We have a deep love and respect for *The News-Item* and the community of Green. We are shocked at the implication we would do anything illegal or unethical. Outsiders, with no regard for our beloved town, are trying to tear down years of positive work."

"Don't let their statement get to you," Walt said from his makeshift office in our boardroom. "The truth will be told. They know what they've done. And you have the respect of many people in this town—even if you are a newcomer."

All the distractions sidetracked our romance, but I found his presence comforting and relied heavily on his intellect and instincts to make key decisions.

I sat down with him and Duke at the bank one morning soon after the IRS visit. "I need to talk about selling the paper," I said. "This chaos threw me off course. To complicate it even more, Eva's interested in making an offer and needs an answer."

"Don't do anything immediately," Duke said. "Let the dust settle till the end of the year."

"You're going to have a tough time closing on this deal with so much litigation pending," Walt said. "Need to let the courts decide how much money you can recover from Lee Roy and maybe even Dub and Chuck." Everyone in town knew about Lee Roy's arrest. Not only had we covered it in the paper, but also it was one of those topics people liked to stand around and talk about.

"Absolutely," Duke said. "Pay the interest on the line of credit and see what happens. Then you can renegotiate with the bank."

When I left the meeting, I walked directly over to the department store to see Eva. "Things are in too much of a mess to give you the answer you need," I said. "The timing is not right."

She took it with grace and smiled. "Well, that settles it. Can I count on your support for mayor, ma'am?"

"You have my vote." I shook her hand firmly.

Heading to the paper, I ran into Walt. "I'm still not sure I did the right thing," I said. "I like Eva so much. She would make a fine newspaper publisher."

Before he could respond, I continued. "But maybe she can still buy the paper if she gets elected mayor. Green's small enough that the job is really more part time than full time. For heaven's sake, Mayor Oscar was a barber on the side."

"You did the best you could," Walt said. "Quit worrying about it. It'll work out."

One way or the other, I had not sold the paper. I also had left the Asheville paper hanging. "I halfway hope they will beg me to take the job," I told Marti on the phone. "And I halfway hope they'll hire someone else."

I started taking walks in the evening, trying to sort things out in my mind. I needed fresh air and time to think.

When I first moved out to Route 2, the pitch-black, country darkness scared me. Everything seemed so spooky. I half expected something to jump out of the bushes. Over the months, I became familiar with the road. I would take my flashlight and strike out. These walks were intended to be brisk aerobic exercise for my over-stressed body, but they wound up being strolls where I kicked rocks and enjoyed the stars.

As Thanksgiving approached, something new seeped into my soul on these treks—peace.

"Thanks for that, God," I said, looking up at the night sky. "This is a little hard to believe, but I might actually get it. I get that you're speaking to me through all of this. I really do need you in my life. It just took me awhile to figure that out. Thanks."

I couldn't quite get over how people prayed for me, talked about depending on God, and were certain that God had important work for me to do. They didn't preach at me. They just laid it out there for me to take.

Sometimes I walked down toward Pastor Jean's church at night, stopping for a drink of water and a brief visit. "I've been thinking about my mother," I said one night. "How much her faith meant to her. I'd climb out of bed in the mornings and climb into her lap. She'd be reading her Bible, always, every morning. She always went to church. Always gave thanks for the blessings God had given us."

I paused and looked at Jean, who sat patiently. "I'm not sure how this will play out, but I've got to try to pray something a little deeper than 'help.' And I'm ready to come back to church."

"We'll be glad to have you, Lois."

One night as I set out from my house, Chris pulled up in his pickup with his three dogs, bringing a cake his mother had made me in appreciation for rescuing Mannix. I put it in the kitchen.

"Would you like to take my nightly walk with me?" I asked. He looked taken aback and then quickly recovered.

"Sure. That'd be great. Can the mutts come along?"

I felt more at ease that night than I had since long before the controversies with Major and Lee Roy and the McCullers had erupted. The dogs were busy the entire time, dashing into bushes and barking or running ahead. I had never exchanged more than a few sentences with Chris, and he turned out to be both funny and thoughtful.

"I'm sorry I never got to any of your games," I said, embarrassed.

"Oh, no problem," he said with a big smile. "Next year you can watch us win state. Those fighting Green Rabbits are pretty tough."

"They must love you," I said. "I noticed how close you all were at the downtown social. You probably keep them in line but still have fun."

"They're great kids, mostly. Lots of them don't get much attention at home. They have to keep their grades up to stay on the team, so that helps."

"Do any of them get kicked off?"

"Not if I can help it," he said, pausing to pat all three dogs that had run back to check on us. "They're young, deserve another chance. As my mama would say, they haven't made it over fool's hill yet."

He rubbed his shoulder absently. "The other day a guy with a sprained ankle was having a contest to see who could jump farther in the locker room using his crutches. Just before I stopped the challenge, I decided it was a teachable moment. I won, but it sure made my arms sore."

I laughed.

"I bet you'll have a great season next year," I said. "Iris says most of your starters will be back." It made me sad to realize I would not be there to see a game.

As we got back to the house, I grabbed a couple of bottles of water and cut the cake. We sat in the porch swing and visited for an hour more, talking about the new fence he had put up to keep Mannix, Markey, and Kramer under control, speculating on the route for the proposed highway and debating who would win the mayor's race.

"Let's do this again," he said. I smiled and waved when he drove off.

Our friendship developed slowly that next

231

month. We walked together many evenings, and occasionally he called.

"What do you think about the paper starting a college scholarship fund in Matt's memory?" I asked one night.

"He was a great boy," Chris said. "That would be a nice way to honor him and Iris Jo."

"I also want to see if I can help Katy get to college, instead of beauty school," I said. "She's got the makings of a great journalist. I don't want her to spend her life doing the wrong thing, just because it seemed easy when she was sixteen."

One evening we sat close in the porch swing, both wearing sweatshirts on the chilly night.

"I'm thinking of a big children's Christmas party at the country club," I said. "For all of the low-income kids near downtown. That could be a way to introduce them to something special and to let the town see diversity in action."

"You are amazing," he said. "Just plain amazing. That brain of yours is always working. You are something." And he reached out and gave my hand a squeeze.

His support helped as I tried to move beyond bad things that had happened.

"The Lee Roys and the Big Boys of the world are nothing compared to the Helens and the Jeans and the Katys," I said. "And the Chris's." I thought about my first dinner with Eva, who had just made the runoff election for mayor, and how she had told me that we must do something with what we are given.

"Katy loves the notion of being a crusader. I wonder how I might spend my life crusading for good—and if I have the energy to do that."

"Sure you do," Chris said, draping his arm around my shoulders. "You're doing it already with *The News-Item*. You have your own little army down there. Those folks would do anything for you."

He was a bit in awe of the newspaper business but didn't hesitate to tell me when he disagreed with something the paper had done. "I do wish, though, you could crusade for a little more school sports coverage."

Sometimes when other people wanted to talk about the paper, I tried to change the subject, knowing I could be defensive. But Chris was different. He praised and criticized and asked questions in a straightforward way.

I certainly admired his work as a teacher.

"I'd be in the federal penitentiary if I had to stay in a classroom all day with those kids," I said. "How do you do it?"

I was joking, but he took the question seriously. "I just feel called to do it. I like those kids, and I hope most of them like me. It's good work, the Lord's work. After Fran died, I realized how important it was to do something that mattered with my life."

We had not spoken about his wife, and the little I knew about her came from Iris Jo. She grew up nearby, also taught at the high school, and fought her cancer fiercely. At some level I wanted to ask questions and complete the picture that had formed in my mind. On the other hand, I wanted to keep their marriage separate from my friendship with Chris.

"I'm really beat tonight," I said. "Thanks for the company, but I need to get up early in the morning."

"Me too." He seemed as uncomfortable talking about his wife as I was. He stood up and gave me a peck on the cheek. "I'll say good night then."

"Good night."

As he took long strides across the yard, I practically ran into the house.

The next evening when I left the office, it was dark and I was alone. I caught a glimpse of movement out of the corner of my eye, and for a moment I thought it was Chris. Once in a while he would stop by the paper, usually to drop something off for Iris Jo or to talk to Tom about a football story. I was uncomfortable with the way I had rushed him off last night, and I thought he might have picked up on it.

As I turned with a smile, I realized it was not Chris, but Lee Roy Hicks with a sneer on his face. My heart immediately began to race. I felt so safe in Green that I never took any of the precautions I had taken in Dayton. I fumbled for my keys and my cell, knowing my pepper spray was on the kitchen counter at home.

"Lee Roy!" I said in a shrill tone. "What are you doing here?"

"Well, Miss High and Mighty, I thought I would drop by to tell you hello and say thanks for ruining my life." He stepped closer to me, and I backed up, until I was pushed up against my car, with his body nearly touching mine.

"You shouldn't be here," I said.

He looked around. "Come in here and act like you can take over this town. Where's all them friends of yours now?"

He was rambling, and I could smell liquor on his breath.

"Lee Roy, you don't want to do this," I said. "Go home and sleep it off. We can talk about this in the morning."

"Maybe I want to talk about it now. Everything was going great until you came along, sticking your nose in everybody's business, stirring things up at the country club, letting high school kids sell advertising, like it was some menial job. This was supposed to be my paper." His voice got louder. "My paper. The McCullers promised it to me, not some city girl who didn't know squat about Green, Louisiana."

Although terrified, I felt sorry for him. As Aunt Helen would say, he had squandered his talents.

He was smart and well-liked and ambitious. He probably could have run the paper or been mayor or any one of a dozen other things if he hadn't been such a louse. But this louse had me pinned up against a car, and I needed to do something.

Using a move my brothers taught me when I went off to college, I kneed him as hard as I could. He groaned and grabbed at his crotch and stumbled back, before falling to the ground, stunned.

At that moment, Rose walked out of the Holey Moley and squinted my way as her eyes adjusted to the darkness. "Lois, is that you over there?"

"Oh, thank you, God. Yes, Rose, it's me. Please call the police. Quick!"

Within a few minutes, the parking lot was full of people. "It's going to be all right," Rose said, touching my arm. "Everything's fine now. We're here."

A police officer put a handcuffed, mumbling Lee Roy into a squad car. "She won't get away with this," my attacker muttered.

Stan pulled in from one direction, and Iris Jo and Chris from another. All of them rushed up, looking terrified. Chris gave me a big hug and kept his arm around me. "Are you all right?"

Feeling a bit dazed, I assured everyone I was fine. "Where did you all come from?" I asked. "What are you doing here?"

Come to find out, Helen's friend had heard the call on the police scanner. She had phoned Iris Jo, who had called Chris and Stan. Within a few minutes, Linda appeared, alerted by Rose, followed closely by Tammy, who had heard it from her former brother-in-law, who was a Bouef Parish Sheriff's Deputy. Alex and Tom popped up after receiving a call from the clerk at the police station. I figured it would only be a matter of minutes before Katy and her mother drove up.

I looked around and, suddenly, smiled the biggest smile I had ever smiled.

"Supper's on me at the Cotton Boll," I said.

19

For the first time in twenty years, Green Missionary Baptist Church soloist Mary Lee Bryan will be unable to participate in this year's performance of Handel's Messiah, *following the district football finals during which she lost her voice while cheering for the home team from the sidelines. Get well, Mary Lee! And Hallelujah to the Green High Rabbits!*

—*The Green News-Item*

Kevin came to visit, close to despair.

"What are we going to do?" she asked. "These sorts of living conditions cannot go on. We must do something. We've put this off as long as we can."

She was responding to an upsetting news story about a house fire in the Lakeside Annex. A space heater exploded, and two children and their mother had died of smoke inhalation. A baby and elderly grandfather had survived, but were in critical condition. There were no smoke detectors in the house.

The next week we had a nearly unbelievable story about an infestation of bats forcing another family out of their home. The couple who rented the house from Major Wilson's property company called the fire department about their problem. A parish inspector found a filthy mess, including forty-five decomposing bat carcasses, dead birds, and a large number of hibernating bats. The parish declared the house unlivable. The couple was frantic, not knowing where they were going to find an affordable place to stay.

Kevin and I had discussed this neighborhood off and on for months, and her concern had escalated during our girls' night out dinners.

"Let's talk to your parents about it," I said. "They'll help us figure it out. Why don't you all come over to my house for supper tomorrow?" The Taylors had been the first people to have me over for dinner, and I had a feeling of peace again as we visited over one of the casseroles from my freezer.

After eating, Kevin and I cleaned up while Pearl and Marcus chatted. We returned to my kitchen table to come up with a list of possible tactics.

"We somehow have to weave this neighborhood into the overall life of Green," Kevin said. "It stays separate now. There's such a high crime rate over there, compared to the rest of Green. Young thugs hang out on the corners and harass good people. Many of the residents are poor and uneducated. They do not even begin to know how to take care of their property." Passion and pain were apparent in Kevin's voice as she spoke of the very neighborhood where she lived.

"And some of the folks are elderly," Kevin's mother said. "They don't have anyone to help them with their housework, much less their yards. And half of them are afraid to leave their houses because the neighborhood is so dangerous."

I pulled out a notebook and listed possible resources. At the top of the list was *The News-Item*. "We can do news coverage and write editorials about the efforts. And we can contribute to a smoke-detector fund to get it going."

We knew the fire department would help install the smoke detectors and educate residents about their importance. We hoped the police department might beef up patrols in the area to cut down on loitering and crime.

"Add the Lakeside Neighborhood Association. We're ready to jump on this effort at a moment's notice," Mr. Taylor said. "List the Green Forward group, too. For downtown to reach its fullest potential, nearby neighborhoods need to flourish."

"And I'll get the South Green Merchants Group involved. I don't want to hear complaints again that we shut them out," I said. "It's high time we pulled more areas together. We should be one community, not a bunch of factions."

"You are absolutely correct, Miss Lois," Marcus said. They stood to leave.

"Thank you for that delicious supper," Pearl said. "I especially enjoy a meal I don't have to cook."

Just after the Taylors pulled out of the driveway, Chris pulled in to say hello. He stopped by regularly, even on evenings we did not go for a walk, staying for a few minutes after he finished up at his catfish ponds.

Dishing up leftovers for his late supper, I told him what we had been discussing. I enjoyed bouncing ideas off him and increasingly found myself wanting to pick up the phone to tell him something funny that had happened in town.

"This could be something good for Green, don't you think?" I asked.

"This community needs more efforts like this," he said. His quick agreement reassured me the idea was not off-base. "I can get the football team and other students to help with a spruce-up day in the neighborhood."

The idea seemed to grow instantly in both our minds.

"Maybe Grace Community can paint a house for someone who is disabled. Maybe even challenge other churches to do likewise."

Representatives of all the groups gathered downtown at the paper one evening with an enthusiastic buzz in the room.

"This can make an awesome Christmas present to the community," Katy said.

Her friend Molly quickly jumped in. "Katy and I can organize the party for the children at the country club. Tammy will help us, won't you?"

"I'd love to," Tammy said. "We'll give those kids a party like they've never seen—not to mention what the country club has seen."

With all of this going on for the Lakeside Annex, we received notice that the state and federal highway departments were close to finalizing the much-awaited route for the new North-South Interstate Highway—a path that went squarely through my yard and through the land of several of my Route 2 neighbors.

"The preliminary drawings show the highway cuts right between the church and my house," Pastor Jean said, when I called to ask if she had seen the letter. "Folks are already in an uproar out here. And not only out on Route 2, but also in town. I've had two dozen calls already."

For a few days, I set the notice aside, thinking it would be years before the road could be built. However, it ate at me, thinking about what it might do to the area and wondering if the bureaucrats who put it together knew the havoc they wrought on the lives of ordinary, tax-paying citizens.

"People are panicking," Iris Jo said during a newspaper planning meeting. "They think the government can come in, bulldoze their homes, and leave them with nothing."

"Sounds like the same thing the tenants in Lakeside are worried about," Molly said. I glanced at her, impressed with the observation.

"Let's write some editorials and pull together a community forum," Tom said, quite serious about his commentary duties. "Why don't you check with that woman preacher and see if we can have it out there?"

Pastor Jean agreed immediately when I called. "You can definitely have the meeting at the church. This is a neighborhood issue, and the church needs to take part. I would appreciate it if you moderated the discussion."

I invited a representative from the Louisiana Department of Transportation and Development, our congressman, candidates for mayor, and the head of the Green Chamber of Commerce. We publicized the event in the paper, and Tom wrote nearly poetic editorials.

"People must make their opinions known and fight for the best route for our area," he said. "It's high time that the highway department listened to real people, the tax-paying, bill-paying public."

The night of the meeting the little church was packed, from choir loft to people squeezed into every pew to an overflow crowd in the foyer and out onto the front lawn. There was almost a carnival atmosphere, and I realized the energy that could be generated when people rallied together behind a cause. The audience was extremely diverse, made up of long-time farmers in the area, elderly widows who were scared to death, young couples who had built homes out in the country or who had remodeled family houses, people who sold produce out of the back of their pickups, and a few wealthy landowners who had lots of acreage with timber or some sort of cash crop.

"Good evening," I said, leaning over the pulpit. The microphone squealed, and several people shouted, "We can't hear you."

I adjusted the mike and tried again. "Good evening. I'm your neighbor, Lois Barker, and we're here tonight to talk about the proposed path of Interstate 69. As you know, the Green area is part of two choices for this interstate's corridor through North Louisiana. As a businesswoman and resident of Green, I do not want to block this project. It has the potential to help our area—our entire region—greatly."

As I said that, several people grumbled, and one man yelled out, "I do. I want to block it. We don't need that kind of progress."

A handful of people clapped, while a few others said, "Shhh! Let her talk."

"However," I plowed on, wondering what I was doing up here, "I do not want to see the highway ruin my neighborhood, hurt my neighbors, and take away the charm of our community. So, we must let our voices be heard and suggest the government choose an alternate, less disruptive route, which will require flexibility in Green. I sincerely hope this does not sound like I'm trying to push the interstate off on others, make it their burden."

"Why not?" someone in the audience yelled, and a few people laughed.

Many people applauded, and there was a hum in the room as people talked to those around them. Trying to keep people quiet, I introduced the guest speakers and moderated the question-and-answer period. I was impressed at how many people I could call by name as they raised their hands.

When I had arrived in Green eleven months ago, I had thought it a fairly dull place without much going on. Now it seemed that every time I turned around I had something else to deal with. As I looked out at the crowd that night, I realized how even in small communities there was always some sort of drama playing out, the daily exchanges between friends and neighbors and the efforts of trying to change what might need changing and keep what was worth keeping.

I took advantage of the gathering to invite

people to participate in our Lakeside Annex cleanup and party day. "As most of you know, we've scheduled an event for the first Saturday in December—'Green's Gift to Green.' I hope you will come and help us make this a better place to live."

In the next week, groups kept calling, offering to do all sorts of useful things. I also had an unexpected visit from Kevin, who was so busy at her clinic that she seldom stopped by my office during the week. "I had some business I needed to take care of downtown and wondered if you might want to get some lunch," she said.

A weird déjà vu feeling hit me, as I remembered a similar conversation with Ed just over a year ago. "Sure," I said. "What's up?"

Just as Ed had done, Kevin put me off until we were seated at the catfish restaurant on the south side of town, a sure sign she wanted to talk more privately. "I've decided to buy some of the houses in the Lakeside Annex, and I need your help," she said. "I've talked to your banker friend Duke, and he's good to go, but I need you to vouch for me with the bank's loan committee."

"No problem," I said, thinking there was something wrong when the committee needed me, a newcomer, to vouch for someone who had grown up here, whose parents were community leaders and who probably made five times more money than I did.

I looked up from the menu and smiled. "That's great. How many houses are you buying?"

"Twenty-five."

I had expected her to say two or three. "Twenty-five? Excuse me, but did you say twenty-five?"

"Yes, I said twenty-five, and, good Lord willing, that's only going to be the starting place."

I shook my head again. "Kevin, did you just tell me you're buying twenty-five houses in the Lakeside Annex?"

"Yes, Lois, I did. Now listen! I don't have all day here. God has blessed me with a great upbringing and a wonderful medical practice. I make a good living, and I want to use it to help others. They're not very expensive in the shape they're in, and I've been in touch with one of the out-of-town owners. He's happy to unload them. I can get all of those for the price of one big fancy house on the lake."

"That's fantastic," I said. "What an idea!"

"This is an investment for me, too, and Daddy says he can help me manage them. These houses are bound to go up in value as the highway comes through and the lake continues to develop and as we fix up that area."

"Can I buy one?"

"Sure, you can buy a half dozen if you want. I figure there are sixty houses in that neighborhood, and I intend for all of them to be owned by the current tenants or by me within the next ten years. Except for the ones you buy, of course."

"And I thought I was a goal-setter," I said, picking at a hush puppy.

"There's more. I'm working out a plan at the bank to help some of the tenants buy their houses on the lake, the ones by my folks' house. Duke thinks we might be able to work this out as part of the mediation with Major Wilson's case. He says it's a certainty the Cypress Point development is dead and that Major needs to look for a way to buy some goodwill with the Feds and with some of his constituents. To top it off, apparently I'm not the only person of color who tried to buy a house in Mossy Bend and was turned down for no apparent reason. His whole real estate business could crumble if he can't work this out."

"Not to mention he can still be prosecuted for violating the Civil Rights Act," I said. Several times I had tried to talk Kevin into telling her story for the newspaper, but she had declined, getting firmer with each mention of it. I had even wanted her to look at houses in white neighborhoods and report on the reactions when she asked about buying something.

"Not interested," she had said. "I need to put my time and energy into something more productive."

Apparently she had.

I walked around the table and gave her a hug, something I seemed to be doing everywhere these days. "You are one amazing woman," I said, "and I am proud to have you as my friend."

"Right back at you," she said, and we walked out grinning.

God smiled on us on "Gift" day, and by now I was willing to admit it was God's doing.

The weather was clear and cool, but not too cold to paint. The sky was as blue as I had ever seen it. Nearly a thousand people picked up litter, cleaned out yards for disabled and elderly people, and painted houses. About two hundred smoke detectors were installed and tested, with Tom keeping a careful list so we could follow up. The South Green Merchants Group happily agreed to participate, cooking hamburgers and hot dogs for volunteers and residents. During the middle of the afternoon, church buses and the nursing home van pulled up and took eighty-five children to the country club for their party.

Kevin and I ran to Kevin's house, changed clothes and met them there.

Katy, Molly, and Tammy dressed as elves. They had completely outdone themselves. There were two Santas, one black and one white, and the children climbed onto their laps, one right after the other. I wasn't sure who the white Santa was, but I thought the other Santa looked like the pastor from the First Methodist Church. Our photographer volunteered to take pictures of the children to give to their parents, and Alex was his assistant, keeping track of names and addresses.

High school girls painted dozens of faces with

candy canes and Christmas trees and stars. The club had donated sugar cookies to decorate and had set up tables with icing and sprinkles for the project. They also had hooked up the sound system, and representatives from youth groups around town led karaoke-style singing of Christmas carols that was as tender and funny as anything I had ever seen.

Just before it was time to load the kids up and take them home, I caught Kevin's eye and both of us started crying. If I live to be as old as Aunt Helen and with as full a life, I may never have a moment more abundant than with that group of excited children scrambling around the Oak Crest Country Club.

The next morning I headed into Grace Community Chapel for my second worship service in a year. I would not have skipped church that day no matter how tired I was.

During the time for prayers and praise, I slowly stood up, nervous but certain of what I needed to do. "I want to say thank you to God for bringing so many loving people together yesterday to help make Green a better place to live and for blessing me so richly with so many wonderful friends in my life."

"Amen," several people said, and we bowed our heads to pray. When I looked up, Chris, sitting over on the side, caught my eye and winked.

Right after church I threw a thank-you party at

my house, inviting the people who helped get Green's Gift to Green going, my growing group of friends who were always ready to help. For so many years I had wanted my home to be open and available and the kind of place where people liked to gather. I had wasted enough time.

Chris volunteered to fry a turkey for the occasion, a local tradition that I had not yet experienced. He also grilled chicken and sausage for what turned into a regular feast. I had insisted, apparently for naught, that everyone had worked hard enough already and did not need to bring anything. Homemade food, from Iris Jo's famous seven-layer dip to Tammy's coveted cream corn, poured in. Tom, who I didn't even know could cook, brought something called a turducken, an odd combination of a turkey, duck, and chicken. Even Katy and Molly came in with a sack, giggling as they pulled out a large bag of Skittles, several packs of bubble gum, and a frozen pizza.

I asked Pastor Jean to bless our meal and felt my heart swell again as I looked at the bowed heads around the room.

Right as she was wrapping up her lovely prayer, the phone rang, but I ignored it. The room was totally quiet, and I was annoyed by the interruption.

"Miss Barker," a man's voice said on the answering machine, "this is Jim Mills, up in Shreveport. Get back to me as soon as you can. I have a good offer on your newspaper."

20

*The ladies auxiliary of Green United
Methodist Church will hold a
bake sale to raise funds for its mission
project this year: a trip to south Louisiana
to restock church pantries damaged by the
recent storm. All canned goods and
Cajun seasoning are needed.*

—*The Green News-Item*

The possibility of making a lot of money on the paper excited me. I couldn't pretend otherwise. But it was hard to enjoy the thought of wealth when most people in town were either peeved at me or terribly hurt.

The day after the call I walked through the front door of the paper to be greeted by one of the looks Tammy was famous for. "Well, good morning to you, too," I said, refusing to be bullied, and spoiling for a fight.

"How could you?" she asked, following me into my office. "How could you plan to sell the paper and not tell us? We're your friends, for heaven's sake."

That afternoon Katy came in with the same question and her old surly voice. I had forgotten how snide she could be.

"How could you, Lois? How could you do this to the people who love you so much? I thought you cared about Green and about this paper and, and, and about me!"

I finally quit trying to explain and simply apologized.

"I'm so sorry. I never meant to hurt your feelings. I do care about you, but I'm not from Louisiana. I got this paper as a responsibility from my friend who died, and I had to come down here and take care of it. It's time for me to go."

That sounded hollow even to my ears, as though it had been a big drag. Nothing could be further from the truth. This year in Green had been a great experience. But I was not a small-town woman, nor a southerner.

The news of the Sunday phone call flew around town faster than a story broadcast on cable news channels. Katy had run out of the house crying, Iris Jo had given me an "I thought I knew you better" look, and Chris had looked completely puzzled. Tammy grabbed her purse and left.

Pastor Jean broke the ice slightly by saying, "Amen" loudly and starting the serving line. By the end of Sunday afternoon, I had explained myself so many times that I was hoarse—and I still felt ashamed. Many of the guests weirdly ignored it, almost as though that would make the call evaporate.

"I guess I'm a little disappointed you didn't mention it," Chris said with a somber look on his face as he was helping clean up. "I thought we were . . . well, getting close."

"I didn't know what to do," I said. "This whole situation, this whole year . . ."

"Well, keep me posted," he said, quickly loading his grilling gear and driving off.

"Help," I whispered after everyone had gone. "Lord, give me wisdom. Show me what to do."

A regional chain was willing to pay top dollar for the little *Green News-Item*. Our accounting problems had been cleared up, and we were making more money than I realized.

The corporate buyers suggested we had potential to make more if we were managed better, which seemed fairly haughty but was probably true. They had other properties, as they called them, in the area and wanted to add *The News-Item* to their holdings.

Everywhere I went that week I felt as though people were whispering and pointing, so I pretty much stuck to the house and the office. Of course, the newspaper wasn't much of a refuge.

Some people in town forgave. Rose, for example, hated to see me go, but was matter-of-fact. "You've got to do what you've got to do," she said when I ducked into her shop.

Linda took it much more personally. "I don't like it one bit," she said. "Seems sort of tricky to me. But it is a sure thing." She had been through enough hard times to believe you don't walk away from a sure thing.

Eva was so wrapped up in her hotly contested mayor's race that she did not have much time to acknowledge the sale. "I'm a businesswoman," she said. "I would have liked a shot at it, but you must have had a good reason for your decision."

Iris Jo also understood. "I remember the first day I spoke with you on the phone," she said. "You had barely even heard of Green, Louisiana, and sure didn't plan to move here. You've done a lot of good things in your short while here."

One thing I wanted to do was to get some things in place before the sale to help a few people. I had not seen Walt in a few weeks, and I invited him to my house for dinner, telling him to put me on the clock because I needed to ask him some business questions. I felt bad that I had not made more time for him because I did like him. I knew he had expected more out of our relationship, and I thought I had been rude.

That night, while dinner was cooking, we sat in the porch swing, and I tried to decide how to open the conversation. We had not dated enough or gotten close enough for this to be a breaking-up speech. It was more of a clear-the-air talk.

Finally, I swallowed hard and started. "Like most of the people I care about," I said, "you deserve a great big apology."

He looked a bit taken aback and then laughed. "Oh, we're the town martyr now, are we?"

I looked more closely at him and realized he knew exactly what I was getting at. "Walt, you're one of the nicest people I know. I love hanging out with you, and I don't know what I would do without your legal advice. I am very sorry that something else didn't develop between us."

"It still can," he said.

"No, I don't think so," I said. The truth was I was leaving and had no interest in a long-distance romance. And somewhere deep inside me, I knew if I were to try to keep a relationship going, I wished it could be with Chris. He was in my thoughts far more than I cared to admit.

Once I had my personal talk out of the way, I launched into my list of legal questions, eager to hear Walt's answers. "I need to know how much leeway I have in some staffing decisions. What kind of contract can we draw up to assure job security for a few people?"

He wasn't overly optimistic.

"You're just like some of my will clients who want to control things from the grave," he said with a laugh. "It'll only work if the buyers want the paper badly enough. Then we might have some clout. Let me do some research."

As he was leaving, he leaned over and hugged me for a long moment. "You're a special person,

Lois Barker," he said. "It's my great pleasure to know you."

Just at that moment, Chris drove by on the way back from his catfish ponds, with his usual honk and a wave. He almost turned in, then seemed to realize I had company and went on. I had only seen him in passing since the day of the dreaded phone call. I had been gone a lot, including trips to Shreveport to work on the details of the sale and lots of time at the office. I knew from reading the sports pages that Chris was tied up, helping out with the basketball team. He had not stopped by. I was crushed.

The next day Walt called, excited, saying he had found several precedents for what he called the "continuity arrangement" I wanted. He thought we could work it out.

I immediately went to Iris Jo's desk, told her what I was trying to do, and asked if she would be willing to take over as business manager, handling Lee Roy's old duties, plus a handful of others. "I realize this is a little unconventional, since I'm leaving, but there's no one in the world more capable of keeping this place going."

She balked at first. "Lois, I'm to blame for not catching all the malfeasance that was going on. And I'm not qualified for a job like that. Besides, the new owners will want their own person in place."

I countered every statement with one of my own.

"Iris Jo, I'm begging you to at least consider the

job. It will be good for you and for the paper. And I have a few more ideas, but I need you to help pull them off."

I had her attention. "We need to interview Linda and consider bringing her on to take your old job. She has lots of business experience, is a hard worker, and we know we can trust her with the paper's money."

Iris smiled. "Besides, it's a missionary act to get her away from Major," she said.

"I also want to bring Molly on as a part-time intern to help you and Linda and to learn more about the business. Watching her these past months, I suspect she has a head for business and needs a place to realize it. I am taking a risk, spending someone else's payroll money with no guarantee they will keep everyone on." I swallowed hard. "But I have to try."

Maybe I had a guilty conscience, but I wanted to leave things in better shape than I had found them.

My negotiations were punctuated by the last days of the mayoral campaign, an intense race that thankfully seemed to take people's minds off of my business dealings. Without having had a true mayoral election in decades, the race was something of a novelty. Louisiana had an ancient election law calling for Saturday elections, left over from the days when people from the country came into town for the day, and Election Day felt like some sort of holiday.

Eva's opponent, a banker who worked with Duke, was a good man. But I happily pulled the lever for my friend, knowing she would do a great job. Our newspaper had endorsed her and took credit when she won, but it wasn't because of the editorials. She had won by four votes, which we figured were mine, Tammy's, Iris Jo's, and Tom's.

Through the next few days, other things came together. Duke and I went over the numbers, which looked outstanding. Walt looked at contracts with Jim, the business broker. I met the buyer's representatives at Jim's office and shook hands on the deal. I had a seven-day grace period to sign the papers, and we set a meeting for the next week, four days after Christmas. Walt and Jim and I went over the details again, and I left, overwhelmed at how much money would head my way at the first of the year.

I hoped to see my brothers for Christmas, but with the sale about to close, it didn't work out. Several people invited me over to eat the holiday meal, but I still felt as though I had wronged them and decided to stay home. I even skipped Christmas Eve services at church, skittish about not being welcome there any more. I had a few presents from my brothers and one from Marti to open.

I thought of last year's Christmas Day, when I had staffed the city desk in Dayton. At least this was better than that.

Late in the afternoon, just as the sun was setting on the clear, cold day, I went for a long walk, needing to decide where I was headed after I sold the paper. While I didn't have to leave town immediately, I knew I did not want to hang around and watch someone else run my newspaper. And Asheville was still open and needed an answer.

As I walked back up the road into my driveway, Chris's dogs came running out to greet me, frisky in the chilly air. When I looked up, Chris was standing at my front door with a plate covered in aluminum foil and a small gift.

"Oh, there you are," he said. "I thought you were avoiding me and wouldn't answer the door."

I laughed, even though I didn't feel like laughing, and invited him in.

"Merry Christmas," he said, leaning over and giving me a kiss on my forehead. "I heard you didn't get to go home for the holidays, so I brought you some of my mama's world-famous turkey and dressing and a piece of pumpkin pie and a little present."

"But I don't have a gift for you," I said, embarrassed.

"Not a problem," he said. "I've had a great time just getting to know you these past few months. That's been a gift for me. I'm sorry I've not come by sooner."

Since it was too cold to sit on the porch swing,

we settled on the sofa, once more sitting close. When I opened the package, I found an unusual piece of old green pottery. "That was my grandma's," he said. "I noticed you like that stuff." He motioned toward my collection lining a weathered bookcase.

I turned the piece over to look at the mark on the bottom. It read, "Route 2 Pottery."

"They used to make it down the road there years ago," he said, pointing toward the crossroads, "where that little old church house is." I turned and gave him a huge hug and a quick kiss. My stay in Green had many moments that would rank in the never-forget category, and this was close to the top, his gift, his visit, his friendship.

"I know we haven't been friends for long," Chris said, "but I hate to see you go. It's going to feel mighty lonesome out here on Route 2. I'm happy for you, though, getting a good price for the paper and all."

Tears came into my eyes, and I looked down at the small green pitcher. "It's really hard to leave, but it's what I need to do."

"I wish you all the best." He stood to go. "Maybe our paths will cross again some day. Maybe you'll come visit us from the big city."

The next day at work I tried to finish everything that needed doing and began to put my few personal belongings in a box. I decided to leave two pieces of art as a gift for Molly and Katy. They might not appreciate them now, but someday they would.

I left work after everyone else, planning to drive up to Shreveport and spend the night. My closing appointment was extremely early, and I didn't want to hit the road so early—plus, I felt the need to distance myself from Green before I took this next step. As I walked through the lobby, I noticed that someone—Katy, no doubt— had painted the name of the paper at the bottom of the list of death notices on the window, complete with a skull.

At first I was so irritated that I started to demand she clean it off, but then I stopped. Was I killing *The News-Item*? Would corporate owners take good care of this paper and care about it and care about Green? I loved my little paper.

Aunt Helen popped into my mind. "What are you running away from?" she had asked. What *was* I running away from?

I had friends here, people who loved me. I had something going with Chris. My work was fulfilling. I was helping others make a difference in the community. I wanted to learn more about the faith and hope I'd begun to have, and I could do that here.

So what if the summers were hot? I did have air-conditioning.

"Help," I whispered, sitting down on the steps of the paper. I looked around, hoping to see a rainbow as I had done that day in Zach's office or to hear the word "stay."

I laughed at my foolishness, and a wave of peace washed over me.

I went back into my office, unpacked the box and called Walt. I knew I needed to tell the broker Jim immediately that I had changed my mind, but I wanted to see where I stood legally first.

Walt hooted when I told him. "I knew you'd never sell that paper," he said.

"You did not."

"I really did," he said, "but, whew, you came pretty close, didn't you? We've got a mess on our hands."

"But I have a grace period," I said. "We haven't closed on the deal."

"I'll take care of it for you," he said, pausing, "even if you did dump me."

"I didn't dump you," I said, "and thanks for handling it. I owe you big time. I'll sing at your wedding or speak at your funeral or help you get elected governor. Just get me out of this."

I was being awfully flippant for someone giving up a nice wire deposit to her bank account and making a fairly big media corporation very angry. I couldn't help it. I felt so good.

"And, Walt, I'm going to need your help in changing some legal papers right away."

"I'll call you at home as soon as I wrap up with

Jim and the corporate guys, and we'll do whatever we need to do."

My next call was to Duke, who also laughed loudly.

"You nearly fooled me," he said. "I couldn't believe you'd sell your precious *Item*, but I had my doubts these last couple of days." He volunteered to come over to my office right away to help me sort out the changes, especially what I needed to tell the bank.

The next day I spent holed up at my house, meeting with Walt and Duke and working out a million details. I didn't want to go downtown because I knew that Iris Jo and the others thought I was in Shreveport selling the paper. I wasn't ready for them to know differently.

One of my more unpleasant chores was calling the publisher in Asheville, severing that option. He was gracious and congratulated me. "Running your own newspaper is something very special," he said. "Enjoy every minute of it."

Zach, however, was peeved when he got the word and called me later that day. "You're burning bridges here, Lois," he said. "You really should follow through on this position."

The day after that, December 31, I breezed into the newspaper with three boxes of doughnuts. I had never breezed anywhere before, but today I definitely breezed into *The News-Item*. Someone had washed the newspaper's name off the window, and I smiled.

"Mighty cheerful today, aren't we?" Tammy asked. "Didn't figure we'd see any more of you around here. See you brought some doughnuts to celebrate your big deal."

"You got it," I said. "Would you get everyone to gather around in the newsroom?"

Grumbling, Tammy made the rounds through the newspaper plant, pulling everyone together in the news area, just as we had done the day I started. I set the doughnuts on a desk and looked everyone in the eye—people I had not known only a year ago, people who meant so much to me today.

"I think most of you have forgiven me for being an idiot," I said. "I may not deserve that forgiveness, but I accept it with great appreciation."

I wasn't sure how to continue and thought I probably should have written my remarks down. I could tell they figured I had come to say "goodbye" and were ready for me to get on with it.

I took another deep breath. "I have backed out on my deal and, if you'll have me, I intend to stay in Green."

Everyone rushed at me, laughing and crying and talking all at once. I held up my hand.

"I need to tell you something else. I have set a profit-sharing plan in motion that will make each of you owners of the paper, in line with how many years you have been here. This paper would not be the paper it is without each of you, and I can't thank you enough."

If I thought the room had been wild a few minutes before, I was wrong. It exploded with people hugging me and cheering and yelling, "Happy New Year." It was a very fun moment.

Just after lunch, Walt and his father appeared in my office. Walt told me more about how he had "gracefully" backed me out of the deal. "In the end, while the corporate brokers were aggravated," he said, "it was just business to them."

His father held out an envelope, addressed in the old-fashioned script that I recognized as Aunt Helen's. "As you know, Walt and I have been the newspaper's lawyers for many years, and I was also Helen's personal attorney. She asked me to give you this when you decided not to sell the paper." He smiled.

I opened the envelope to find the deed to the house on Route 2 and a two-word note. "Welcome home," it said.

That night I slipped into the back pew of Grace Community Chapel. Katy and I had visited for a long time earlier in the day, and she had invited me to the New Year's Eve services, being led by members of the small youth group. I was delighted to see her friend Molly there and several teens I did not recognize. The lights were turned down low, and candles flickered on each windowsill.

Katy had not told me she was giving the main message, but I was not terribly surprised when she stood up. She spoke of what a hard year it had been for her and others and how life sometimes just didn't seem fair.

"But so much good comes to us, and we have to learn to appreciate it and not waste any of it," she said. "God calls each of us to do wonderful, special things with our lives." She announced the scholarship fund we were setting up in memory of Matt, and Iris Jo looked as though she would cry for the second time that day.

"Most of all," Katy said, staring straight at me, "I have realized that all you have to do is your part. You do your part, and watch what God will do. Grace and peace to each of you in the New Year."

Just as the service ended, Chris looked back, saw me and moved into the pew beside me. He touched my arm. "I'm glad you're staying," he whispered.

"So am I."

ACKNOWLEDGMENTS

Green News-Item Golden Pen Awards Given

The Green News-Item would like to thank its wonderful community correspondents, who regularly contribute such great local news to your newspaper.

The Golden Pen Award for outstanding "*News-Item* Community Item" this year goes to Suzanne Zitto. Close runners-up are Paul Christie, Alisa Stingley, Ginger Hamilton, Martha Fitzgerald, Mary Ann Van Osdell, Teddy Allen, David Christie, Mary Frances Christie, Craig Durrett, Carol Lovelady, Eleanor Ransburg, Sarah Plunkett, and Alan English.

In addition, the staff thanks those faithful newspaper supporters—Alisa Stingley, Kathie Rowell, Barbara Montgomery, and Paul Christie. Thanks, too, to Etta Wilson, Paul Franklyn, Barbara Scott, and Jenny Youngman.

Discussion Questions

1. *Gone to Green* is told in first-person through the character of Lois Barker. How would you describe Lois to a friend? What are her best characteristics, and where does she falter?

2. Early in the story, an unexpected "gift" from a colleague confuses Lois. What causes her misgivings? Is it a mixed blessing for Ed to pass along a business with strings attached? Did he believe Lois would move down south? Have you ever been thrilled and upset by the same event?

3. Lois makes an important choice early in *Gone to Green*, setting in motion a variety of other changes. How might things have turned out if Lois had chosen to stay in Dayton? Why do you think Lois decides to move to Green? Do you find life's decisions are usually clear-cut or require a struggle? How do you make decisions?

4. The community of Green plays a key part in this story. How would you describe the town to someone about to visit? What is special about it? What needs improvement? What is the role of downtown?

5. Green changes Lois, and she changes the town. In what ways does it have the greatest impact on her life? How does she most change

the community? List some of the changes that occur in *Gone to Green* and consider how you might have handled them. Do you find it easy to deal with change? Have you ever gotten tangled up in change? Is Lois bothered by change?

6. If you were a community correspondent for *The Green News-Item*, what would you write about?

7. What does Lois's attitude about Green tell us about her as a person?

8. Living out on Route 2 affects Lois in unexpected ways. What might have been different had she lived in a new condo on the lake? How is her rural neighborhood a community within a community? Do you think people differ by region?

9. As the owner of the newspaper, Lois encounters a host of challenges. If she were not a journalist, how might her life as a Green newcomer have been different? What are the biggest obstacles she faces?

10. Lois gets to know a variety of people in Green, including young Katy, Aunt Helen, Dr. Kevin Taylor, Eva Hillburn, Pastor Jean, Walt, and Chris. How does each influence Lois?

11. In what ways are Dub and Chuck McCuller, Lee Roy Hicks, and Major Wilson similar and how do they differ? What impact do they have on Lois?

12. How would you describe the journey Lois is on? What parts do career, geography, relationships, and spirituality play in it? Have you considered how different areas of your life affect one another?
13. What advice might you give Lois as her journey continues? Are there areas in your life where you might want or need to grow or change? What will Lois have to deal with as she continues to develop?

Center Point Publishing
600 Brooks Road ● PO Box 1
Thorndike ME 04986-0001 USA

(207) 568-3717

US & Canada:
1 800 929-9108
www.centerpointlargeprint.com

ML   1/10

Dear Parents,

As the creator of Go! Go! Sports Girls and the founder of Dream Big Toy Company, I would like to thank you for giving your child the gifts of reading and healthy life-skills.

Healthy habits start early. I created Go! Go! Sports Girls as a fun and educational way to promote self-appreciation and the benefits of daily exercise, smart eating and sleeping habits, self-esteem, and overall healthy life-skills for girls. Author Kara Douglass Thom and illustrator Pamela Seatter have taken this dream a step further by creating a series of fun and educational books to accompany the dolls. Now your child can Read & Play.

The books have been written for the child who has begun to read alone, and younger children will enjoy having the stories read to them.

I believe every child should have the opportunity to Dream Big and Go For It!

Sincerely,

Jodi Bondi Norgaard

Jodi Bondi Norgaard

For our very own sports girls
Grace, McKenna, Kendall, Jocie Claire,
Kaelie, Maia, and Michaela,
and their brothers Peter, Ben, Blake,
and Alex, who inspire us every day.
— JBN, KDT, PS, SRB

First published in 2014

Series Editor: Susan Rich Brooke

Text © 2014 by Kara Douglass Thom

Illustrations © 2014 by Pamela Seatter

www.gogosportsgirls.com

Library of Congress Control Number: 2013951458

First Edition

8 7 6 5 4 3 2 1

This book was printed in 2015 at Luk Ka Packaging Co., Ltd.
in Street No. 98, Lijia Road, Henggang, Longgang Dictrict,
Shenzhen, Guangdong, China.

ISBN 978-1-940731-03-2

Go! Go! Sports Girls™

Swimmer Girl Suzi's Story

Winning Strokes

Written by Kara Douglass Thom

Illustrated by Pamela Seatter

Dream Big Toy Company™

Suzi sat on the starting block, her feet dangling just above the water. She wasn't allowed to get in the pool until her coach arrived. With her big toe, she tapped the surface. Ripples of water circled her foot.

Suzi loved swimming. Her mom said that when she was a baby, the bathtub was her favorite place to play. She loved splashing and blowing bubbles.

As soon as she was old enough, Suzi joined her big sister, Hana, for swim lessons. Hana swam as smoothly and swiftly as a fish. She had already earned a spot on the community swim team.

Swimming Through Time

Pictures found in caves show early humans swimming. It looks like what we call "dog paddling" today.

Ancient Romans built swimming pools as meeting places. People swam to stay cool and clean off.

British knights were required to swim in body armor! Today's "wet suits" are made of rubber.

In the early 1600s, the Emperor of Japan made all the schoolchildren learn how to swim and race.

In the 1800s, there were swim clubs and swim meets in the United States and Europe.

Swimming was added to the Olympic Games in 1896. Now there are more than 30 swim events.

At every swim meet, Suzi cheered for her sister. While Suzi learned freestyle, backstroke, breaststroke, and butterfly, Hana won shiny ribbons—blue ones, red ones, and white ones—for those same strokes.

Suzi struggled to keep her head in the water and to breathe to the side when she swam freestyle. But Hana could breathe easily on both sides when she swam. The only time she lifted up her head was when she touched the wall at the end of a race.

Different Strokes

These are the main swimming movements, known as strokes.

- In freestyle, your arms paddle through the water one at a time. Your legs stay straight out behind your body in a flutter kick.

- The backstroke is similar to freestyle, but you do it on your back. Backstroke is the only stroke that you start in the water, instead of diving in from a starting block.

- In breaststroke, you pull both arms under the water at the same time, from the front of your head to below your chest. Your legs kick like a frog.

- The butterfly has an overhead arm stroke and a fast dolphin kick.

Suzi looked forward to her swim lessons every week, but sometimes she came home frustrated. On the ride home one night, she was extra quiet.

"I have one piece of bubble gum left," Suzi's mom said.

"I want it!" Suzi perked up.

"Okay, but first tell me what's on your mind."

"Swimming," Suzi said.

"What about swimming? Do you still like your lessons?"

"Yeah," Suzi said quietly, hoping she could get the gum already.

"But?" Her mom glanced at her in the rearview mirror with a raised eyebrow.

"But I want to race like Hana," Suzi said.

"You'll be able to race soon."

"Really? On Saturday?"

"Oh, no. You have to pass the swim test first."

Suzi sighed. Her mom handed her the bubble gum.

"That's never going to happen," said Suzi. "I'll never be able to keep my head down like Hana does."

"Never?" her mom asked. "Remember when you first started lessons? Your arms and legs went in so many directions that you ended up swimming in a circle."

"Yeah, and Hana said I looked like a squid!" Suzi and her mom giggled at the memory. It seemed like such a long time ago, but it was really just last year.

"Now you're more like a dolphin," her mom said. "And even dolphins need to come up for air."

Hana's ribbons were shiny and silky. They hung in a cluster on her bedpost like a rainbow waterfall: blue, red, white, yellow, and green.

Once, Suzi asked Hana if she could have a ribbon. "Just one," Suzi had said. "You have so many!" Hana didn't even answer—she just glared. Suzi knew that meant "no."

From then on, Hana kept a close eye on her ribbons and counted them often to make sure none were missing.

Suzi kept going to her swim lessons and working on her strokes. The next year, she took the swim test—and passed!

Finally Suzi was on the swim team! She was so proud to wear her swim team jacket and go to meets with Hana.

Most of Suzi's heats were early in the meet, and Hana's were later. This meant Suzi could compete and watch her sister race, too. Hana kept on winning colorful ribbons. And now, Suzi's own rainbow waterfall of ribbons began to grow.

Ribbon Rainbow

Ribbon colors may vary at different swim meets, but here's what they usually mean:

Blue: 1st Place
Red: 2nd Place
White: 3rd Place
Yellow: 4th Place
Green: 5th Place

What to Wear

To swim in a race, you'll need a one-piece swimsuit, goggles, and a swim cap.

When the swim season was over, Suzi still practiced swimming. But Hana didn't go with her as often as she used to.

"Where's Hana tonight?" Suzi asked her mom on the way to the pool.

"She's busy studying for a big history test," her mom said. She glanced at Suzi in the rearview mirror. "Bubble gum?"

"No thanks," Suzi pouted.

When Suzi met up with her friends at the pool, she forgot about wanting Hana to be there too. And once she started to swim, she forgot about everything else besides swimming.

She swam freestyle—her favorite stroke— to warm up. Then she worked on some drills.

First, she practiced stroking with just one arm. Next, she used a kickboard and fins to work on her kick. After that, she swam the whole length of the pool on her side with one arm reaching out past her head. She liked that drill most of all because it made her feel like a mermaid.

She practiced breaststroke and butterfly, and finally, her strongest stroke: backstroke.

At the start of the next swim season, Suzi and Hana signed up together. After the first week of practice, Suzi saw that her off-season pool time had paid off. She was swimming in a faster lane, the one right next to Hana's lane.

And when it came time for the first meet, the coach moved her up to the next level: Hana's level.

Now Suzi would be racing against her sister! She felt excited and thrilled and nervous and scared, all at the same time.

Kick It Up!

Swimmers sometimes use fins or flippers, a kickboard, a pull buoy, and hand paddles to practice kicks and strokes.

Suzi sat on the starting block, her feet dangling just above the water. She adjusted her goggles over her swim cap. Then she dipped in her foot to feel the water and watched the ripples it made.

Hana sat on the starting block beside her. They were swimming in the final heat for freestyle.

"You'll do great," Hana said. "Good luck!"

Suzi just smiled. She was too nervous to talk.

The warning bell went off. Suzi got into position. Her toes gripped the block beneath her. With her knees bent and her arms hanging, she leaned over as far as she could without falling in. When the starter blew the warning whistle, Suzi was ready to spring forward.

"Swimmers, take your mark!" boomed the starter.

Suzi bent her knees and steadied her arms. She wanted to get a fast start, but she didn't want to fall in or have a false start.

Buzzzzzzz!

The swimmers dove in. As her arms churned through the water, Suzi kept her eyes on the black line at the bottom of the pool and didn't look at anyone else. She just swam as fast as she could to the other side. She touched the wall and caught her breath.

Then she looked up at the scoreboard and saw...third place! She had touched the wall just after Hana.

Suzi couldn't wait to get her white ribbon at the end of the meet and hang it in her ribbon waterfall. It felt great to be in the top three. And it felt right to finish behind her big sister, who would get a red ribbon for second place.

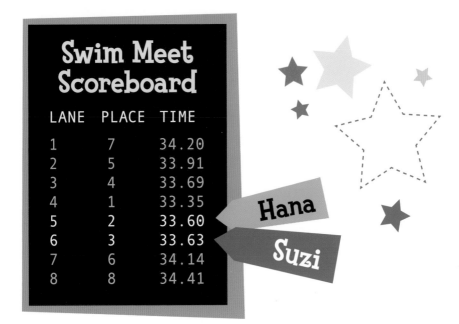

Swim Meet Scoreboard

LANE	PLACE	TIME
1	7	34.20
2	5	33.91
3	4	33.69
4	1	33.35
5	2	33.60
6	3	33.63
7	6	34.14
8	8	34.41

Hana

Suzi

Racing Rules!

- *You must wait for the starting signal to begin the race.*
- *You must stay in the same lane you start in.*
- *You can't swim the whole race under water. Your head must come up within 15 meters (50 feet) after the start, and after each turn.*
- *Walking on the bottom of the pool or tugging on the lane ropes is not allowed.*
- *You can't wear anything that helps you float or swim faster.*
- *Some part of your body must touch the wall at the end of the race.*
- *When swimming breaststroke and butterfly, you must touch the wall with both hands at once. This is known as "two-hand touch."*

Suzi's next race was breaststroke. Hana had already raced in an earlier heat and made the finals.

This time, Suzi didn't do as well. She liked the frog kick, but she still needed to work on her arms. Getting them in the right position while she came up for air was tricky.

She came in last place, feeling like Suzi the Squid all over again.

As Suzi reached for her towel, she felt Hana's arm on her back.

"Brush it off," Hana said. "Backstroke is next. That's your best stroke."

Suzi knew she was as good at backstroke as her sister. Hana had more power because she was older and a little stronger, but Suzi's stroke was smoother. When she practiced, she could feel her arms slice through the water.

Now it was time to get ready. Suzi clung to the side of the starting block. Her knees were bent to her chest, and her feet gripped the pool gutter. She turned to her left and saw Hana two lanes over.

Hana smiled and gave her sister a thumbs up. Suzi smiled back and then...

"Swimmers, take your mark!"

Buzzzzzzz!

Ready, Set, Flip!

If a race is more than one length of a pool, a swimmer does a "flip turn" by rolling or somersaulting right before the wall. Then she pushes off the wall with her feet to swim in the other direction.

Suzi pushed off, streamlined, and kicked under water. She broke the surface and took strong, powerful strokes. When she saw the flags above her, she started counting her strokes. Her hand touched the wall exactly when she thought it would.

Then Suzi looked up and saw that she had touched the wall first. *First*. Before everyone else in the pool. Even before Hana.

For the first time, Suzi had swum faster than her big sister.

Would Hana be angry?

Suzi was barely out of the pool before she got the answer to her question. Hana came running and picked her up in a great big bear hug.

Back at home, Suzi put her new white ribbon on the bedpost with her rainbow waterfall. But she didn't put her new blue ribbon there. That ribbon was special. She hung it up in its own place, next to her mirror.

Every morning, she would see it there and remember her big sister's big hug. Then she would smile at her reflection... and look forward to the next swim meet.

Here's What Suzi Learned:

- Be proud of how far you've come, and don't compare yourself to others.

- The more work you put into something, the more you can improve.

- Win or lose, if you do your best, you can feel good about the outcome.

- You can be happy for the people who finish ahead of you.

Swimmer Girl Suzi's Healthy Tips:

- **Pair up.** Never swim alone. Make sure a lifeguard or adult is always watching.

- **Eat up.** Natural snacks like orange slices or pumpkin seeds give you more energy than sugary snacks.

- **Drink up.** Even though you're surrounded by water, swimming is hard exercise and can leave you thirsty. Make sure you drink water, not sodas or sugary drinks.

- **Cover up.** When you swim outside, remember to protect your skin with waterproof sunscreen.

- **Rest up.** Get lots of sleep every night, especially before a swim meet.

Dream Big and Go For It!